CAPTAIN KATHRYN JANEWAY OPENED HER MOUTH BUT WAS INTERRUPTED BY A SCREECHING BURST FROM HARRY KIM'S CONSOLE.

The rat-a-tat sound of static followed, and she winced at the volume.

"Someone is attempting to contact us," Kim told her, yelling to be heard over the noise.

"On screen," Janeway shouted back.

The image of the wormhole was replaced by scratchy static. An unintelligible voice boomed. Kim worked frantically, and after a few seconds the voice began to form words, and a shape manifested on the screen.

"—to the *Starship Voyager*. Repeat, please acknowledge if you are receiving this!"

The image solidified—dark, sleek, short hair, pale skin, a ridged brow, a noble face. The hair along Janeway's arms and at the back of her neck lifted, as if she were seeing—and hearing—a ghost.

"Telek R'Mor," Janeway whispered.

For she knew the voice and the visage that now appeared on the screen. They belonged to a man who was now dead—or was he?

When were they?

STAR TREK VOYAGER®

CLOAK AND DAGGER

DARK MATTERS

BOOK ONE OF THREE

CHRISTIE GOLDEN

POCKET BOOKS
New York   London   Toronto   Sydney   Singapore

This book is a work of fiction. Names, characters, places and incidents are products of the author's imagination or are used fictitiously. Any resemblance to actual events or locales or persons living or dead is entirely coincidental.

An *Original* Publication of POCKET BOOKS

POCKET BOOKS, a division of Simon & Schuster, Inc.
1230 Avenue of the Americas, New York, NY 10020

A VIACOM COMPANY

STAR TREK is a Registered Trademark of Paramount Pictures.

This book is published by Pocket Books, a division of Simon & Schuster, Inc., under exclusive license from Paramount Pictures.

ISBN: 0-671-03582-7

First Pocket Books printing November 2000

10 9 8 7 6 5 4 3 2 1

Printed in the U.S.A.

This book is dedicated to the memory of DeForest Kelley

Thank you, Bones.

PROLOGUE

TRAMP. TRAMP. TRAMP. TRAMP.

The echoing sound of booted feet striding in unison on the smooth stone floor of the Senate chamber was a familiar one to Jekri Kaleh. She could not count the number of times she had entered this room to stand before the gathered Senate, and occasionally, as was the case today, even in the presence of the Empress herself. Sometimes Jekri had entered in triumph, more rarely in shame.

But always, the Romulan head of the Tal Shiar came with her head held high and her bright silver eyes gleaming.

Today, her heart pounded with excitement in her abdomen, though her face was nearly Vulcan-like in its lack of expression. It was not becoming for the head of the Tal Shiar to gloat.

Tramp. Tramp. Tramp-tramp. Tramp.

Inwardly, Jekri frowned. Their honored guest, the reason for the assembly, was out of step. Such things bothered her, but there was no help for it. And besides, if what her guts were telling her was true, the ambassador could do skip-and-turns all over the hall and no one would mind.

With perfect timing—except, of course, for the ambassador—the honor guard Jekri led came to a halt before their Empress, the Senate and Proconsul, and the Praetor.

The Senate chamber was a rainbow of pageantry and old opulence. The heavy stone trapped coolness here, despite all attempts at warming the place during the winter months. The acoustics were perfect. Not a whisper went unnoticed. The huge traditional banners of every important Romulan *hfihar*—noble house—hung from the high stone ceiling. No disruptors or other energy weapons were permitted. Only ancient weapons could pass the scrutiny of the unsmiling guards at the entrance to the long hall. Here was welcomed the sharpened blade of the sword, the heavy stone of a club stained dark green with blood spilled centuries before, the slim, elegant lines of the dagger—the *kaleh,* from which Jekri Baseborn had taken her name.

The Empress, a slim woman still in her late adolescence, was clad in red. Unlike most of her subjects, who preferred a practical, short haircut, the Empress wore her thick, dark hair long. The Empress dictated fashion; she did not follow it. The ebony tresses were now gathered up atop her head and decorated with precious stones that matched the scarlet of her long, off-the-shoulder garment. Her father had been a proud warrior. The Empress did not herself know the ways of weapons, but she was canny in her ability to find and promote those who did.

To her right stood the Praetor—tall, handsome, his black eyes missing nothing. The Proconsul, as usual, sat with the senators. Normally Jekri Kaleh would take her place on the Empress's left, as was her right as chairman of the Tal Shiar. But today she stood before her liege, not beside her.

"Welcome, Little Dagger," the Empress said in her cool, husky voice. Only she and the Praetor could call Jekri so. Not even the senators dared use a diminutive to the leader of the Tal Shiar. "It has reached our ears that you have brought us a very important visitor."

Jekri stood arrow-straight and brought her clenched right hand to her left shoulder in a precise salute.

"Honor ever to the Empress, the Senate and Proconsul, and to the Praetor. I have indeed found and brought to you a most honored guest. He is—" Jekri hesitated for the briefest of instants. "He is an ambassador from a far distant place. Ambassador Lhiau, pray you, salute our Empress and our Praetor."

Ambassador Lhiau strode forward with enough arrogance for twenty praetors. He was tall, as tall as a Romulan, and similar to Jekri's people in form.

But his hair was thick, wavy, and pale, and there was no distinguishing curve to his ears. When he bowed, it was almost mocking.

"Greetings, Your Excellency. Praetor. The noble Romulan Senate and Proconsul. I hope my arrival heralds the dawning of an age of enlightened discourse between your people and mine." The voice was rich, sonorous even. But the little smirk ruined the otherwise courteous speech.

"And which people might yours be?" replied the Praetor. His voice was high and slightly whiny, unfortunate for a man who spent so much time in public, but his people knew and respected what he did. "Your race is unknown to us. I can only surmise," he said, with a sidelong glance at Jekri, "that our Tal Shiar has learned something remarkable about you. At first meeting, I fear that I can see nothing remarkable."

Lhiau's smile remained, but his eyes went cold as chips of ice. "Perhaps when I am finished, you will think better of your Tal Shiar—and of me."

"Perhaps," said the Praetor. "But you had best continue, Ambassador, and not waste the time of the Senate or the Empress—or myself."

Now the smirk did fade, and Jekri thought curses. She hoped that Lhiau would not rise to the bait and would instead plainly state what he had come here to discuss. If this conversation degenerated into an exchange of insults, nothing Jekri said would convince the Empress to hold a second audience with him. The ruler of the Empire was a proud young woman, almost haughty, and during her reign it had become

4

obvious even to the most obtuse senator that she would brook no discourtesy to her royal personage.

"My people, as the estimable Jekri Kaleh has said, come from a faraway place. Very, very faraway. We call ourselves the Shepherds, and you may also use the term, if you like."

"How gracious," purred the Empress. The sarcasm in her voice was palpable. "A faraway place, beings who call themselves Shepherds. You did not tell us that your friend was a spinner of tales, Little Dagger. We would have brought children."

Instead of the outburst of rage Jekri expected, Lhiau merely smiled. "Yes, a tale then, if you like. It's fantastical enough, as I'm sure you'll agree. What would you say, Excellency, Praetor, Proconsul, if you could make a wish and suddenly have a flawless cloaking device?"

That got their attention. The tightness in Jekri's abdomen eased a little as she saw the hungry interest spark to life on the faces of the Empress and the Praetor. Even the Proconsul and the senators leaned forward eagerly, probably unaware that they did so. Jekri sniffed. She had better control.

"A very special, very magical cloaking device," Lhiau continued, playing out the joke of a story being told. Jekri saw that the assembled senators were insulted at the condescension, but were too interested now to indulge their righteous indignation. As she had been . . . .

"A cloak that placed no drain on the ship's energy sources. A cloak that never, ever needed to be replenished. A cloak," Lhiau said, emphasizing this final point, "that did not require deactivation in order to attack?"

"Why, you are truly a teller of tales, Ambassador," said the Empress. "A good storyteller knows his audience—and you clearly know a great deal about our cloaking device. How came you by this knowledge?"

Lhiau wagged a finger at her. "Ah, ah, a good storyteller doesn't tell all his tales at one sitting. I see you remain unconvinced. Perhaps a demonstration?"

He turned to Jekri and nodded. She tapped the communication device on her wrist.

"Kaleh to the *Tektral.*"

"This is the *Tektral.*" It was Jekri's second-in-command, Subcommander Verrak, who answered. For the purposes of the demonstration, Jekri was willing to utilize her personal vessel.

"Prepare to engage the Shepherd's cloaking apparatus on my command." She turned to face the Triumvirate. "With your permission, I would like to activate the viewscreen."

Skeptical, the three most powerful individuals in the Empire exchanged glances.

"You may, Little Dagger," said the Empress.

Jekri bowed, then turned to face the screen that occupied a full wall of the council chamber. The image of the *Tektral,* small, green, and graceful, appeared against a backdrop of white stars and black space.

"The *Tektral* has been fitted with an apparatus given to us by the Shepherds." Jekri gestured, and one of her centurions stepped forward with the device. He bore it carefully, almost reverently, on a small black pillow that set off its deceptively fragile beauty.

The Shepherds' apparatus was like nothing any of them had ever seen. Small enough to fit into the palm of a hand, it was formed of some sort of crystalline material. It seemed to pulse, as if its energy source came from within, making soft shadows dance on the pillow. It looked more like a piece of fine art, carved by the skillful hands of a Romulan sculptor, than anything mechanical. Jekri noted the murmurs of awe and appreciation, carried to her pointed ears by the magnificent acoustics of the building.

"At your word, Empress," Jekri said, "I will give the order for Subcommander Verrak to activate the apparatus."

For a long moment, the Empress could not tear her eyes from the beautiful piece of alien equipment. She was a fine ruler, but she had her vanities, and it was obvious that she ached to caress the pretty bauble.

"Proceed," she said at length, reluctantly lifting her gaze from the device to the screen.

"Verrak, engage," ordered Jekri.

For a moment, nothing happened. The senators fidgeted, talking among themselves. Jekri was unperturbed. Let them wait. Then, so slowly that the eye might have missed it, the *Tektral* began to disappear, as if bits and pieces of it simply melted into nothingness, until it was entirely gone. It took a few seconds for the portent of the spectacle to sink in, but the murmuring ceased and the room fell completely silent as those assembled realized what was transpiring. Jekri could not remember that ever happening before.

The Praetor recovered first. "Computer," he said, the word rough. He cleared his throat. "Computer, analyze the *Tektral*."

"The *Tektral* is not in the area of designated space," stated the computer in its harsh, male voice.

Gasps arose. The senators began chatting excitedly, and Lhiau smirked.

"How can this be?" snapped the Proconsul. "You must have fooled us—teleported it somehow!"

"No, Proconsul," said Jekri. "I give you my word, it is still there. Our sensors simply cannot locate it. And if ours cannot, then rest assured, nothing the Federation can contrive will be able to find a vessel so cloaked. Verrak, fire photon torpedoes in display pattern alpha-gamma-beta."

From out of empty space, three photon torpedoes surged forth. After a moment, two more torpedoes were fired from an entirely different position. Then, finally, from yet a third position, one last volley. There was not the faintest distortion of space to indicate where the cloaked ship was.

Lhiau had not lied. The cloak was utterly without flaw.

For a long moment, no one spoke. What they had just witnessed was inconceivable outside of fantasy—yet they had just seen it with their own eyes.

"Ambassador," said the Empress at last, her voice cracking, "What thing is it you will require of us for this tale made true?"

"Nothing that is beyond the skills and resources of the famous Romulan Star Empire," replied Lhiau. "I want you to help me defeat my enemies. I've heard that Romulans are very good at things like that."

CHAPTER

1

THE SOUND OF HER OWN VOICE SCREAMING BROUGHT Captain Kathryn Janeway wide awake. She bolted upright, gasping for breath. Perspiration was slick on her skin, and her nightgown clung to her.

"Lights," she called in a voice that shook. Her throat felt sore from the scream. She shivered, chilled by the drying perspiration. The nightmare had been particularly bad this time.

She forced herself to take deep, slow, even breaths as she glanced about, feeling foolish even as she sought reassurance that the dream was not her reality. All was as it should be. These were her quarters—home to her now for over five years. There was the huge window. Often, when she had trouble sleeping, which was not infrequent, Janeway would rise, get a glass of cold water from the replicator, and gaze out of that window for a long time. The comforting image of white stars zipping past on the blackness of space sometimes lulled her back to sleep.

But not tonight—or, she amended, glancing at the timecounter, this morning. Her lips thinned and her heart, which had begun to slow, speeded up again. For when Janeway looked out her window now, she saw nothing that brought comfort. She could see only the mystery that had been confounding them since they first began noticing it almost seventeen hours ago—dozens, perhaps hundreds of wormholes.

Like little mouths, they were, she thought; black and mysterious, yawning open for a few seconds, then closing. It was almost—almost—worse than her nightmare.

"Seven of Nine to Captain Janeway."

"Janeway here."

"Captain." Seven's voice was cool and crisp, efficient as ever. "I have some new information on the wormhole phenomena which you and Lieutenant Torres should see."

Janeway had already risen and was reaching for her uniform as she replied, "On my way."

The three women stood together, shoulder to shoulder, in Astrometrics and gazed at the bizarre image Seven of Nine displayed before them.

It was obvious to the captain that the whole thing was starting to get to them. Lieutenant B'Elanna Torres, the half-human, half-Klingon chief engineer, had her arms folded tightly across her chest and was scowling at the images as if her vexation alone had the power to make them disappear. Seven of Nine, who had once been more Borg than human, still had a cold precision in her manner that made Janeway shudder if she thought about it too long. And Janeway herself had to admit that she was growing increasingly angry with this mystery that they seemed nowhere near solving.

A red line wound its way from right to left. Surrounding it were dots of white in varying sizes.

"What are we looking at, Seven?" asked Janeway.

"The red line," Seven said, "is the path that *Voyager* has been following for the past eighteen point six days. The white dots indicate lingering traces of verteron particles. I have graphed them in proportion to the strength of the radiant emanation. By my calculations, none of these wormholes was stable for more than nine seconds."

"But, we've only noticed the wormholes materializing over the past seventeen hours and twelve minutes," said Torres in a voice that was almost a growl. Her temper had been shorter than usual over the last several days, and that was saying something.

"Correct," replied Seven, utterly unperturbed by Torres's irritation. "I took the liberty of expanding the sensor's search patterns to focus on verteron emanations and retraced our route over the past several weeks."

"Good thinking, Seven," said Janeway absently. She always made it a point to acknowledge initiative

12

and good work when her crew showed it, although right now her mind was racing at a thousand light-years a second.

Her gaze traveled the red line that represented her ship's path over the last few weeks. A chill raced down her back as she looked at that red line. She regarded its position of several weeks ago. There were no signs of wormhole activity then. But as the line moved toward the left-hand side of the giant screen, a few of the strange holes in space began to appear, though still far away.

The closer *Voyager* came to its present position, the more wormholes dotted the screen—and the closer their proximity to the ship.

"And these are the most recent ones?" she asked, to confirm her suspicions.

"Correct," Seven replied. "The most recent wormholes are the ones closest to our vessel."

The overall effect was that of a twining, crimson snake being pursued by a swarm of insects increasing in number. It was a fanciful image, one which both Seven and B'Elanna would scorn, but Janeway couldn't shake it. She didn't have to speak with her first officer, Commander Chakotay, on the bridge to know that there were dozens of wormholes opening and closing right this very minute—all coming closer to her ship, all getting larger. She'd seen enough from her window.

"Any new theories?" Janeway asked, not expecting a response. Seven and Torres exchanged glances, but were silent. The nature of wormholes was still something of a mystery, though they were certainly not unknown phenomena. But the plethora of wormholes they were witnessing was unheard of in Janeway's experience. She herself had seen over a hundred. Now, Seven's graph showed many times that number.

"Perhaps," said Torres slowly, "we're entering some sort of field where the wormholes are more frequent."

"The elephant graveyard of wormholes, eh?" Janeway smiled. "It's possible. Though I think it's one heck of a coincidence that our path through this sector is taking us so directly through that field."

She stepped forward, craning her neck, as if simply being closer to the chart would bring her some enlightenment. "No, B'Elanna. Good guess, but no. It's almost more like . . . as if it's cause and effect."

"You believe we are being followed by wormholes?" The scorn in Seven's voice was palpable. Her blue eyes were wide with disbelief.

"When you put it that way, it does sound foolish," her captain admitted, biting back an angry retort. Her emotions, perhaps because of the nightmare, were more raw than usual. "But look at it. Put aside logic for a moment and just . . . look at it."

She pointed. "There—back when they started appearing. See how random they are? Now, let's look here—just a week ago. Much more precise—the wormholes are almost in a line themselves. And now they're all over the place. They're literally surrounding us."

She said no more, and let the other two women

see for themselves. B'Elanna frowned even more, and a growing unease spread across Seven's beautiful face.

They saw it too, now.

And it was scaring them just like it was scaring Janeway, though none of them would ever admit it.

Janeway's headache, banished by her distraction for a few moments, returned, throbbing angrily in the right temple. She resisted the urge to press her fingers to it. Doing so never helped. Nothing ever helped, not the Doctor's too-vigorous massages, nor the medicine he prescribed, nor a trip to the holodeck. And these strange, unsettling wormhole manifestations only made her tension worse.

The mystery was taking its toll on the crew as well, from what Janeway could judge. She'd heard Tom Paris and Harry Kim, normally the best of friends, quarreling rather bitterly after a holodeck jaunt a few weeks ago, and even Chakotay—gentle, strong Chakotay—had dressed down an ensign for a minor miscalculation at the helm the other day.

Torres had been complaining, vocally, about the seemingly endless small things that had been going wrong with *Voyager* lately—a jammed coupling here, a sluggish plasma venting there. Tiny things, but Janeway could sympathize. A thousand little annoyances were sometimes worse than a real crisis. At least with a crisis, you could focus.

And then there were the nightmares.

Just the recollection made her jaw clench. Janeway had not shared her nocturnal terrors with anyone else, not even the Doctor, who would never dream of violating patient-doctor confidentiality. Not yet, anyway. She'd thought about it. If they got bad enough, she'd have to talk with him. A captain's bad dreams could turn into nightmares for her crew if left unaddressed. But right now, Janeway felt that she could handle it. Some things were just too personal—too intimate.

Janeway took a deep breath, held it, and tried to calm herself. Concentration was what was called for here if they were to get to the bottom of this.

She tapped her combadge. "Janeway to senior staff," she said. "Everyone meet me in my ready room in five minutes."

"These late hours are wreaking havoc with my beauty sleep," quipped Ensign Tom Paris as he entered the ready room. His eyes were bleary and his grin looked forced.

"Yeah," replied Torres, without even looking up. "You look like hell, Tom."

"Why, thank you, sweetheart, and might I return the compliment?"

Tom's voice was hard and there was no humor in it, despite the words. B'Elanna frowned and opened her mouth.

"Ensign. Lieutenant." Chakotay's own tone of voice was just this side of angry. "That's enough out of you two."

Paris's head whipped up and he stared at Chakotay. His eyes narrowed and his nostrils flared. He looked as though he might strike the commander. Janeway was shocked. She decided that, after this meeting was over, she would send everyone on the senior staff down to sickbay for a complete physical. The strain was taking too great a toll. If her crew was too busy sniping at each other to pull together, they were going to be in trouble if any real danger arose.

"The wormhole situation is perplexing, granted," the captain said, stepping forward easily between her first officer and the blond ensign. "But quarreling among ourselves isn't going to solve it. Everyone take a seat and let's hear Seven's report."

Seven of Nine rose and activated the viewscreen. There, in miniature, was the same graph she had shown to Torres and Janeway in Astrometrics. Janeway listened with half an ear, more interested right now in watching her crew's reactions.

Chakotay's expression didn't change, but Janeway could see the subtle tensing in his large body. Tuvok, as usual, was unreadable. B'Elanna pulled into herself still more, and Paris seemed distracted and unable to focus. Neelix, their usally chippejack-of-all-trades cook, morale officer, and sometime ambassador, looked positively glum at the revelations Seven imparted. Harry Kim was monitoring the conversation from the bridge, where he remained at his post. Only the Doctor seemed his normal self.

"Thank you, Seven," said Janeway, rising as their newest crew member took her seat. "We know that wormholes are natural phenomena, and we are far from the superstitious mariners our ancestors were. There are no dragons in space, but there are mysteries. And I'd say we've got a prime one on our hands. I don't like the look of this. The clustering is too precise to be random."

"I'm no scientist," began Neelix, almost apologetically, "but wormholes are natural phenomena as far as *we're* concerned. Who's to say that someone out there hasn't figured out how to control them?"

Janeway smiled, the first genuine smile to grace her lips in what seemed like an eternity. True, Neelix wasn't a scientist, but he'd stated something they'd all missed, something quite obvious. Good for him.

"Out of the mouths of Talaxians," drawled Paris, but he softened the gibe with a wink in Neelix's direction.

"Of course," said Chakotay. "We've even got an example of that right in our own backyard, back in the Alpha Quadrant. The Bajoran wormhole is an artificial construct. The so-called Prophets are the aliens who created it and live inside it. Dammit, we should have thought of this before! How could we have been so stupid, so—" He slammed his right fist into his left hand.

"Gently, Commander," chided the Doctor. "I would dislike wasting my time repairing any bones you might damage in your self-deprecation."

"Seven," said Janeway quickly before the sniping could escalate, "have you picked up any signs of artificial manipulation of the wormholes?"

"Negative," replied Seven. "Although most activity we might be able to identify would occur at the origin site of the wormhole, not its exit site. The verteron emanations and natural radiation of the wormhole would likely obscure any artificial signals. It is also likely that if any other technology is indeed involved, it is technology with which we are not familiar and therefore do not know how to detect properly. The sensors would need to be reconfigured, and—"

"Does anyone have any idea how sick I am of reconfiguring those damned sensors?" said Torres, her voice rising.

"Does anyone have any idea how sick *I* am of—" Fortunately, Paris's comment was cut off by Harry Kim's voice.

"Bridge to Janeway."

Alerted by the taut edge in Harry's voice, Janeway was all attention when she replied, "Janeway here. What's going on, Harry?"

"There's another wormhole, Captain."

"More wormholes? What a surprise," muttered Paris.

Janeway was taken aback by the heat of the anger that rose inside her. The look she shot Paris would have obliterated him on the spot if she'd had her way. He shut up at once. If nothing else, Paris had developed an uncanny instinct for knowing just how far he could push his captain.

Kim continued, "It's the biggest one yet. You'd better get out here and see this before it disappears."

Her anger evaporated as quickly as it came. Despite the headaches, the bad dreams, the short tempers, Janeway was above all else fascinated by this peculiar display of wormhole activity. And besides, there always remained the chance that one of them would be large enough to travel through—and would open into the Alpha Quadrant.

"Dismissed," she told her crew, unnecessarily. As one, they'd all risen and hastened for the door, eager to see this new development.

Janeway couldn't suppress a swift intake of breath as she stepped onto the bridge. Yawning before her was a huge hole in the fabric of space. Verteron particles, normally invisible to the naked eye, were clustered together in such great numbers at the aperture of the wormhole that they formed a purple, swirling gateway. In all ways, save for the purple tint rather than the blue, it resembled a smaller version of the Bajoran wormhole back in the Alpha Quadrant. The similarity brought quick tears of homesickness to her eyes. She blinked them back.

"It is sufficiently large enough for us to send in a probe," said Tuvok.

"It's big enough for us to send in the *Delta Flyer,*" said Paris, slipping into his position at the conn.

"Try big enough for *Voyager,*" said Kim, startling them all. "I've been monitoring it the moment it appeared, just as I have with all of them. This one's been increasing in size at a steady rate of eight point seventeen meters per second. And we're well past the nine-second timeframe at which all the others have closed."

Janeway caught Chakotay's gaze. He gave her a

slight smile. If this led back to the Alpha Quadrant . . . .

"Tuvok, send in that probe. I want to know where this thing originates." She glanced at Neelix, Seven, Torres, and the Doctor. "You four, report to your posts. Harry will make all information available to everyone as we gather it. You won't miss anything, Neelix," she added, seeing the Talaxian's whiskers droop.

Seven of Nine hesitated a moment before following the other three into the turbolift. Janeway knew of the former Borg's apprehension about returning to the Alpha Quadrant. Here, Seven had a place, a function. *Voyager* was, as she had once phrased it, her "collective." Seven had proved herself willing to die for the vessel and its crew—even to subject herself to Borg control to ensure their safety.

But prejudice was an ugly thing, not completely rooted out even in the twenty-fourth century. Many humans would look at Seven and see not the woman, but the metallic implants in her body. Seven of Nine feared for the sanctity of her haven, and Janeway couldn't blame her.

"The probe has entered the wormhole," said Tuvok. The excitement and tension on the bridge was almost palpable, yet, of course, Tuvok was an oasis of calm. "Preliminary readings indicate—"

He fell silent. Surprised, Janeway craned her neck to regard her security officer. "Yes?"

Tuvok met her gaze. She, who knew that face so well, saw the slight tautness around the brown eyes, the flaring of nostrils that marked quickened breathing. Her own heart began to race and her mouth went dry.

"Preliminary readings indicate that this wormhole originates in the Alpha Quadrant."

Without realizing what she did, Janeway had reached out a hand to Chakotay. He met it halfway, gripping it so hard that the small bones in her fingers ground together. She didn't mind one bit.

It was big enough for the ship to traverse. It showed no signs of collapsing.

And it led to home.

Dimly Janeway was aware that her normally controlled bridge crew was whooping with joy. She shared their delight, but she needed calm in order to continue the investigation. There might yet be dangers lurking inside that oh-so-tempting wormhole. She recalled the organism that had lured them into its maw by posing as a wormhole. That "monster" had manipulated their thoughts, made them feel almost ecstatic about returning home. Only Seven, Naomi Wildman, and the Doctor had resisted its siren song.

Janeway's temple throbbed, and she gasped softly, involuntarily. Well, if nothing else, she knew that what lay before them was *not* that same creature. She sure as hell wasn't feeling ecstatic right now.

She opened her mouth but was interrupted by a screeching burst from Kim's console. The *rat-a-tat* sound of static followed, and Janeway winced at the volume.

"Someone is attempting to contact us," Kim told her, yelling to be heard over the noise.

"On screen," Janeway shouted back.

The image of the wormhole was replaced by scratchy static. An unintelligible voice boomed. Kim worked frantically, and after a few seconds the voice began to form words and a shape manifested on the screen.

"—to the *Starship Voyager.* Repeat, please acknowledge if you are receiving this!"

The image solidified—dark, sleek, short hair, pale skin, a ridged brow, a noble face. The hair along Janeway's arms and at the back of her neck lifted, as if she were seeing—and hearing—a ghost.

For she knew the voice and the visage that now appeared on the screen. They belonged to a man who was now dead—or was he?

When were they?

"Telek R'Mor," Janeway whispered.

CHAPTER

2

HARRY KIM COULDN'T BELIEVE WHAT HE WAS SEEING. The universe must really, really have it in for him.

Nearly five years ago, he had been the one who had discovered the small, ancient wormhole that had linked them via a subspace corridor to this Romulan scientist. Kim had never wanted to see the man again. Not because Telek R'Mor was a particularly unpleasant representative of his race. Quite the contrary. During their brief meetings and conversations with Telek, he had proved himself to be a man of intellect, honor, and conscience. He had done everything he could to convince the Romulan Senate to bring back the crew of *Voyager* as a gesture of goodwill.

The only fly in that ointment had been that Telek R'Mor had lived twenty years ago. The wormhole had cut across not mere light-years, but actual years as well. For Harry Kim, Telek was a living example of how close they had come to getting home, and how impossible such a goal had eventually proved to be.

It had been a bitter draft, and Kim was not pleased to have this particular cup thrust into his hands yet again. It felt almost like a physical slap in the face. Although, he had to admit, it did seem that *everything* annoyed him these days.

In response to Janeway's uttering his name, the Romulan nodded a hasty acknowledgment. Now that Kim looked at him, he realized that Telek was anxious. He leaned closely into the screen and almost whispered his words. Harry's own body tightened with apprehension in response.

"I am taking a grave risk by contacting you, Captain Janeway. But it is imperative that I warn you. This is a trap, Captain—one I intend to see fail."

Janeway pressed her fingers to her temple, as if trying to follow what Telek was saying was giving her a headache.

"What? Telek, I—"

Telek pushed on, stepping on Janeway's confused words. "When I returned from visiting your ship, I found the Tal Shiar waiting for me." He glanced over his shoulder, then continued in a hushed, hurried voice. "They have taken my wife and my daughter. I have not even been allowed to see them. I do not like to speak ill of my government, but their methods . . . ."

"You had no choice but to cooperate with whatever they wanted," Janeway supplied, nodding. A thin line of sympathy creased her brow.

"You understand. I could not sacrifice my family. But I cannot sacrifice you and your people either. This particular wormhole is going to close in a few seconds. But they will make me try again."

"Try what?" Chakotay asked. Harry thanked him silently—that was exactly what he wanted to know.

The intelligent gaze flickered from Janeway to Chakotay. "When they learned what I had discovered about you, the chairman was anxious to capitalize on my knowledge. They have ordered me to locate *Voyager* in order to board it and bring it back through the wormhole. You would be useful to them if you cooperated, but they have no compunction about disposing of you if you resist. If they succeed, they may well destroy the true timeline. Captain, we wrestled with this decision once before. We came to a conclusion that we must continue to defend, even with our lives."

Janeway rose and walked down to the screen. The Romulan's head seemed gigantic; her slim, small frame, even tinier to Kim. "Telek, I agree with you and thank you for this warning, but I need more information. How did you find us? What do you know about this wormhole?"

The Romulan's visage contorted in frustration and anger. "There is no time—" he began, then fell silent, horrified. A small red light began to blink on his console. An instant later, there came an angry pounding on the door and cries in the Romulan tongue.

Oh, my God, thought Kim. *They've detected his transmission.* Even as Kim gaped, Janeway turned to him, her eyes snapping fire.

"Get a lock on him!" she cried.

His fingers fumbling only slightly, Kim did as he was told.

The door to the scientist's room slid open. Harry caught a blur of motion and color as helmeted men and women rushed inside.

"Harry! Get him out of there now!"

Harry hit the controls before the words were out of his captain's mouth. Truth be told, Kim had already been moving toward transporting the unfortunate scientist the moment the door had been forced. Telek R'Mor wasn't slated to die until 2367, and Kim wasn't about to let the Tal Shiar take Telek before his time.

The space beside Janeway shimmered, and the familiar sound of the transport beam whined. An instant later Telek stood, clearly startled, next to the captain of the *U.S.S. Voyager.*

The Romulan guards exchanged stunned glances. Then they snapped to attention when a young, very attractive female strode into the room that until seconds ago had contained Telek R'Mor.

Harry couldn't help it. He stared. She was gorgeous. It took him another heartbeat before he realized that, if the deferential treatment by the guardsmen was any indication, the Romulan female was a personage of great importance.

Telek's quick exit may have confounded the guards, but this new individual sized up the situation almost at once. Pale gray eyes, almost silver, gazed into the screen and fastened on Telek. Harry flinched before the raw hatred and fury in those eyes.

She thinks he planned it, Kim realized. *She thinks he's a traitor.*

"Chairman Kaleh—" Telek began in a trembling voice, taking a half step toward the screen with his hands lifted in a supplicating gesture.

"Your family is dead," said the female R'Mor had called Chairman Kaleh.

"No!"

Kaleh was immune to the raw anguish in the scientist's voice. She lifted a small fist and brought it crashing down on the console. The screen went black.

Harry never thought he'd feel sorry for a Romulan, but as he regarded Telek R'Mor, pity swept through him.

The private quarters of the Federation starship were almost roomier than Telek's entire small vessel. He lay on the bed in the guest quarters to which Janeway had temporarily assigned him and gazed out at the almost incomprehensible openness of space. He supposed he should be grateful that he wasn't in *Voyager*'s brig, though, naturally, there was a strapping young human outside standing guard. This human female Janeway had shown him nothing but courtesy and respect in every single exchange they had had.

But there was nothing of gratitude in Telek's heart. It was filled now with an ache that he knew would only worsen as the dreadful reality gradually set in. He saw only his wife, with her bright smile and lively eyes, and his little daughter, whom he had never yet been able to hold as a father ought.

From what he knew about Chairman Kaleh and from the little he had seen of her, Telek had no doubt but that she would carry out her threat. He wondered if she would take out her anger with him by sending in interrogators to torture Torrith and Rakki before butchering them, or if the murders of his family would be quick and painless. He suspected the former, and the thought brought a little moan from him. His mind went back to the day, so brief a time and yet an eternity ago, when he had first encountered this Captain Kathryn Janeway.

"I am working to reconfigure protocols to penetrate the radiation stream of the wormhole," Telek had told the Federation captain, his mellifluous voice sounding sincere even in his own ears as he uttered the lie as he had been ordered. The woman replied, her voice warm and husky and as richly sincere as his own. He would give them time to think about seeing him, to anticipate the contact that would, they hoped, bring them closer to their own quadrant. It was richly ironic that these lost Federation lambs—if lost they truly were—had found a Romulan wolf instead of a good shepherd.

Shepherd. The unconscious word choice made Telek wince.

"Good night," he had told Janeway, remembering that the ensign who had patched through his communiqué had told him that Janeway was asleep in her quarters.

"Good night," she had replied—a little pleased, a little surprised. Telek frowned. He was not a man to whom deception came naturally, and the more he heard, the more convinced he had become that these people were indeed telling the truth. It seemed impossible, but Telek R'Mor, member of the Romulan Astrophysical Academy and head of a highly classified intelligence research project, had lived long enough—and seen enough—to rarely employ the word "impossible."

He had his orders, and was prepared to execute them. Then he saw these lost, lonely voyagers and all the best-laid plans of the Tal Shiar went up in flames. The clever, yet—Telek felt certain—not calculating Janeway had gotten him to reveal that he had not seen his wife in over a year and had never held his seven-month-old daughter. He had spoken of a price paid—and how unexpectedly high that price had been.

When, to his utter shock, Janeway revealed that they'd figured out a way to transport themselves through his wormhole, Telek had been hard-pressed not to give himself away. He didn't remember what he'd told her to allay her suspicions—some nonsense about "can't permit Starfleet personnel on this vessel," and summoning a troopship to take on the crew if the transport did prove to be successful.

A bad slip, that. What so-called low-ranking scientist would be able to ask for and get a troopship so quickly, even in such an unusual situation? But Janeway, flushed with excitement, had not noticed it.

Then had come the remarkable journey, not just through space but also through time. The regret that he was not able to help these humans. The offer that came to his lips so unexpectedly to warn Starfleet not to send *Voyager* on its last mission. The connection he felt with this small female, with her proud eyes and warm smile.

And the return home, with their precious messages to loved ones enclosed in his hand . . . .

She was waiting for him, troops at her call. He knew her, of course, though he had never met her. His project fell under the auspices of the Tal Shiar, and the face of Chairman Jekri Kaleh was as familiar to Telek—perhaps more so, these days—than that of his wife.

"Chairman Kaleh," he stammered, trying to regain his composure. "What an unexpected surprise. How may I serve you?"

She did not answer him at once, merely turned and gestured outside the room. A tall being entered. His hair was long and pale, and he resembled the humans Telek had just left more than he resembled any member of Telek's own race.

"Who are you?" Telek demanded. Where his ship and the security of his project were involved, Telek R'Mor could be as fierce as any centurion.

"Rude, isn't he?" said the stranger, grinning. "So this is the man I need to see."

"Your orders have changed, Doctor," said Jekri

bluntly. "You are to give Ambassador Lhiau your full cooperation. He is to know everything about the project, up to and including your trip to this Federation vessel."

Telek licked lips suddenly gone dry. "Honored Chairman, would that that were possible. I am afraid I cannot reveal anything about my experience aboard Voyager. All records of my encounter with them must be deleted unread by anyone else, and those who have read them already must be sworn to secrecy."

Jekri's brilliant silver-gray eyes narrowed. Clearly, she was not used to being interrupted or disobeyed, and it sat ill with her. "No such thing shall happen. Do not forget yourself, Doctor."

Outwardly, Telek knew he projected an almost Vulcan calm. Inwardly, his emotions churned like an angry sea. Those records needed to be destroyed. He would not, could not pollute the timeline and risk the Empire. He remained stoically silent. They could kill him for disobeying, but he was resigned to that. His only regret was that, if he died, the messages the Starfleet crew had sent to their loved ones would never reach their destinations.

The chairman continued to regard him. When it became obvious that Telek would say nothing more, she gestured. A centurion stepped forward and inserted a data slip into the console.

The screen came to life.

Torrith!

She was clearly terrified, though she tried to show true Romulan courage. "Greetings, husband," she said, and her voice trembled. "I am contacting you from . . . from a holding cell. Somewhere, I don't know. But the Tal Shiar have informed me that Rakki and I are to be their . . . guests for the time being."

Telek's gaze fell from his wife's frightened visage to the tiny, perfect one of their daughter. Her hair was fuzzy and black, only starting to grow in. Her mouth was small, like a flower bud, and as he watched, she yawned and waved little fists. The soft, cooing noise Rakki made as she snuggled back into her mother's embrace nearly brought tears to Telek's eyes.

"We have been treated well," Torrith hastened to say. "Truly, husband. But I have been instructed to tell you that—" Her dark eyes flashed with anger before she continued. "That our lives depend on your cooperation with the Tal Shiar. Obey them, and we live. Disobey, and we die."

Torrith leaned into the screen, as if she could really see Telek. "Use your conscience, my husband. If it is truly important that you refuse, then Rakki and I will die proudly, knowing our deaths mean something. But if it is not so urgent . . . then I should like to see you hold our daughter, someday."

The screen went black. Telek's throat clenched with unshed tears.

"Well, Telek R'Mor?" He turned to face Jekri, and saw a smirk of satisfaction marring her lovely face. "What is your answer?"

Oh, she was good, this young, beautiful manipulator. She knew that there was no torture that would be worse than what was captured on that screen.

"What is it you wish of me?" he replied, *knowing that with those words, contrary to his wife's wishes, he had utterly forsaken what was left of his conscience.*

"Dr. R'Mor."

Janeway's voice startled Telek out of his reverie, and he rose at once from the bed. She smiled and waved him to a seat. "I hope these quarters meet with your approval."

"They are more than sufficient for a humble scientist such as myself," he replied.

Her face saddened and the smile faded. "I must tell you how sorry I am that we put your family in jeopardy. I had no idea that Chairman Kaleh would so misinterpret what happened. We were only trying to save your life."

"The chairman is young, and makes up her mind quickly," Telek said. All the pain seemed locked within him, in the box that was his heart, and there was no hint of it in his voice. "If she were older and felt she had less to prove, she would have taken the time to listen."

Janeway said nothing. There was nothing she could have said, and Telek found the silence comforting. She rubbed her eyes. Only now did Telek notice the deep circles underneath them. He took a deep breath and deliberately put aside his pain.

"Captain, I must meet with your senior staff. Now that I am here, you may as well benefit from my knowledge. I sacrificed my family to warn you. I would not want that warning squandered."

To her credit, she didn't flinch. Janeway might

have initiated the act that would surely bring about the deaths of Torrith and Rakki, but she had made her best decision under the circumstances and would probably have made it again, given the choice. He admired that.

"Janeway to senior staff. Our guest wishes to meet with all of us in my briefing room. Now."

Telek R'Mor wasted no time. When the last officer had arrived and the door had hissed shut behind her, the Romulan launched into a tale that had Janeway and her crew hanging on his every word.

"First, I must apologize for lying to you during our last encounter. I was under orders, and much could have been jeopardized had I revealed the true purpose for my presence at the apparently ancient wormhole. I shall not do that again. Henceforth, you may trust my words."

He swallowed hard and his dark eyes were bright. Janeway grieved right along with him, but honored his request. There'd be no lies from her, either. It was too late for such trivialities.

"And there is much to tell—I hardly know where to begin. First, you must know that the wormhole by which you contacted me in 2351 was not ancient. It was artificial. Not only that, I created it."

Janeway took a quick breath and glanced at Chakotay. He nodded toward Neelix: *Neelix was right after all.*

"As I said, Chairman Kaleh was waiting for me when I returned from your vessel. She learned everything about my trip, and the government decided it was an opportunity not to be missed. I was given new instructions. No longer was this simple research. My wormhole technology was conscripted by the Tal Shiar for two specific purposes. The first was to locate you again. Such a task was easier said than done. I not only had to locate you physically, I had to determine where you were in the timeline."

"Not just where we were, but when we were," said Paris.

"That is correct, Ensign . . . ?"

"Tom Paris. Captain, the wormhole activity—"

"I'm with you, Tom." Janeway turned again toward the Romulan. "The last several days, we've seen an incredible amount of wormhole activity. That was you, wasn't it?"

He nodded his dark head. "You are astute, Captain. Indeed it was. I began with your last known location and followed the path I assumed you would take to reach the Alpha Quadrant. I had a record from our first encounter of your warp particle signature and reconfigured my sensors to hone in on any trace of it. The chairman's plan was simple and basic. I would locate *Voyager*—the most difficult part of the equation. I would then open a wormhole directly in front of your vessel and the Tal Shiar would send in thirteen cloaked warbirds. These vessels would proceed to fire upon your ship while cloaked, and—"

"Whoa, whoa," interrupted Torres. "Wait a minute.

You're twenty years behind us and even in this time the Romulans can't fire while cloaked."

"B'Elanna!" Chakotay's voice cracked like a whip. Janeway raised a calming hand.

"It's all right, Chakotay. It's too late to worry about telling Dr. R'Mor about the future," Janeway said gently. "He knows too much already and, frankly, may never be able to return to tell anyone. Please continue, Doctor."

"I will address your concerns, Lieutenant Torres, in due course. To continue with the plan: *Voyager* would thus be taken utterly by surprise. I would then open a second wormhole that led directly from ship to ship. Hundreds of Romulan shock troops would storm your vessel, beginning with engineering. It would be a matter of moments, would it not, before you would fall to us in such a scenario?"

Janeway hesitated. Seven of Nine spoke up. "There is no question about it. *Voyager* would fall almost immediately before thirteen warbirds."

Telek swiveled his seat and his eyes widened as he took in Seven's implants. "Are you an android?" he asked.

Seven straightened in her seat and replied haughtily, "No. I am—I was—Borg."

"Borg?" Telek cocked his head.

Despite the seriousness of the situation, Janeway had to smile. "Now that one is a long, long story, Doctor. Suffice it to say that if Seven says something, the odds are it's right."

Telek cleared his throat. "As you will. To continue, once we had seized control of *Voyager*, it would be easy to take her back through the wormhole. The Empire would thus have captured a ship twenty years in advance of anything known."

"The ease with which the Romulans would have been able to study and replicate the vessel is disturbing," said Tuvok. "The Federation of 2351 would have had a difficult time defending itself effectively."

"It was a Romulan dream come true," said Telek. "But it didn't happen that way. Not yet. And if I have anything to do with it, it never will. I did yield to the Tal Shiar to save my family, Captain Janeway. But I never intended to betray you or the timeline. The wormhole through which you beamed me aboard should have remained open. The warbirds were preparing to traverse it. However . . . accidents do happen. Accidents," he amended, sorrow tingeing his voice, "such as my being trapped on the wrong side of the wormhole when it closed."

"But, that's good," said Torres. Everyone glared at her. She didn't seem the least troubled by the nonverbal censure. "Think about it. Telek, from what I've heard, this whole project was your baby. You have the knowledge to create these wormholes."

He nodded. "Yes."

"Then with you here, they're stuck. They won't be able to make another wormhole."

"Would that it were so easy," said Telek. "Once, this was indeed my project, and mine alone. Toward the end, I was given assistants—if you can call them that. My notes were taken and analyzed. Given time, others would be able to decipher the encryption. They could learn to manipulate the technology I designed without me. And believe me, with a prize such as *Voyager* hanging before them with all the allure of fruit ripe for the picking, the Tal Shiar will not give up."

"Forewarned is forearmed," said Chakotay. "So, finding us was your first set of orders. What was the second?"

Telek frowned. "Chairman Kaleh was not the only notable personage waiting for me. With her was an alien from a race I have never seen before. He called himself Ambassador Lhiau and said he represented a race called the Shepherds."

Paris coughed. Janeway didn't spare him a glance.

"For the last several months, the Tal Shiar, Ambassador Lhiau, and I have been working covertly together on my wormhole technology." He paused and took a deep breath before continuing. "You see, Captain, Lhiau tells us that the Shepherds are able to manipulate dark matter."

"Such a statement is highly improbable," stated Seven. "While we can recognize it and have even encountered dark matter nebulas, no known species has been able to properly categorize dark matter, let alone manipulate it. Your doubt regarding this . . . this Shepherd is apparent. It may be well placed. Lhiau must have been lying to you."

The upswept eyebrows lifted in offense as Telek turned to Seven. "You may have met many people in the Delta Quadrant, but I dare say you have not met every species that exists," said Telek tightly.

Seven frowned. "The Borg have assimilated over—"

"I've seen it done!" Telek said, his voice rising. "Lhiau is coy, he will not share the secret of how the Shepherds can do it, but they can indeed control dark matter. They have a device that is able to direct it. The Shepherds have provided us with the technology to create a cloak that is quite literally without flaw. *That,* Lieutenant Torres, is how our ships would have been able to fire on you without decloaking. You would never even have known what hit you until our people began boarding your vessel."

"My God," breathed Janeway. The hairs on her arms lifted. "The ability to manipulate dark matter to suit their needs. No wonder the Romulans wanted to deal with them."

"Such a skill has endless uses," Telek continued. "I'm certain your imagination is racing, Captain Janeway, as mine did when I learned of this. The Shepherds brought other skills to the table as well. That tiny wormhole through which you and I corresponded was the largest one I had been able to create on my own. Thanks to Lhiau, who tells me his people dwell inside wormholes, there is now no limit to the size of the wormholes that I can design and open."

"You know, if you ask me," said Paris, though no one had, "I wouldn't trust this Lhiau and his Good Shepherds for a single nanosecond. Sounds like they're pretty powerful beings—almost Q-like," he added, glancing around the table. "Why would they need the aid of a simple Romulan scientist? No offense, Doc," he added hastily.

"None taken, Ensign. I have asked myself that same question. There is nothing we can give them—their technology is vastly superior to ours, and Lhiau has hinted that his present form is not his true one. There can only be one answer. When the time is right, they will demand their payment for their aid."

The Romulan leaned forward, embracing them all with his soft-spoken words. "And when that dark hour comes, I feel certain that the price will be so high, so terrible, that it will destroy us all."

CHAPTER 3

JEKRI HATED THE TINY, UTILITARIAN *TALVATH*.

It was dark and cramped, and filled not with tributes to battles and victory and weapons and art but peculiar tools and measuring devices. She didn't know how Telek R'Mor had spent so long a time here without going mad. Then again, perhaps he *had* gone insane and broken under the strain. Perhaps his loneliness was so profound that he had bonded with the humans, bonded so deeply that when he next got the chance, he abandoned his wife, daughter, and Empire to be with them.

Jekri frowned. She didn't like that scenario. It called for far too much compassion, and as far as the chairman of the Tal Shiar was concerned, compassion was a waste of energy.

She slumped in front of the console, idly reaching

out a finger and punching up information. None of it made sense to her, not even the information that hadn't been encrypted. She was not one for equations and theories. She was for action and conspiracies, for the subtle word whispered here, the knife in the back there. Jekri Kaleh had not survived being born in the alleys of the poorest province on Romulus to waste her time with mathematics and scientific babble.

"Chairman," came the voice of her second-in-command, Subcommander Verrak. Jekri straightened and composed her face before turning around.

"Yes?"

"The Empress, the Praetor, and the Proconsul will grant you an audience now."

She nodded. "Send in the ambassador."

A few moments later, Lhiau stormed into the room. His mere presence seemed to send a charge of electricity through the air. He tossed his fair hair and sneered at her.

"The time for reckoning has arrived, Jekri Kaleh. You've bungled this one brilliantly. I look forward to working with your replacement. So tell me, what do they do to failed chairmen?"

"I wouldn't know," replied Jekri tightly. "I have not failed. And as for your working with someone else, believe me, Ambassador, I would be just as happy to never look upon your arrogant face again. But we must work together if we are to achieve our common goals. This bickering between ourselves is pointless."

Jekri turned back to the console, took a deep, steadying breath, and thumbed the controls.

The three visages Jekri wished to see least in the universe appeared on the screen. All of them looked furious. Jekri had earlier wanted to face them in person, to defend herself as a Romulan ought. Now, she was just as glad that there were light-years between them.

To her surprise, it was not the Proconsul or even the Praetor who spoke first. It was the young Empress, rising from her throne and striding toward the screen with anger on her perfect features.

"Jekri Baseborn," snarled the Empress. "You dishonor all Romulans with your carelessness!"

Despite herself, Jekri flinched at the insult. She hid the gesture of weakness by inclining her head deeply in obeisance.

"Your Excellency," she said, "no one could have predicted Dr. R'Mor's actions. His family was in custody. He knew their lives depended on his actions. Until the moment of his defection, we had no reason to believe that Telek R'Mor was anything but a loyal servant of the Empire."

"Clearly, not as loyal as you had thought," said the Praetor in his thin, high voice. "Perhaps it is time to reevaluate *all* so-called loyal servants of the Empire—beginning with the chairman of the Tal Shiar!"

"No!" Fear was in her voice, and Jekri hated herself for that. Beside her, Lhiau laughed, nastily. "No, Praetor, my honor is my life." She swallowed, and for the first time since she had formally cast off the name of her illegitimate birth, she deliberately referred to it.

"I had nothing before the Empire gave me a chance to prove my worth. I have worked, planned, killed for the Empire to earn this position. Without it, I am nothing. I would no longer be Jekri Dagger, but merely Jekri Baseborn. Think you for a single moment, any of you, that I would risk throwing that away for some misguided scientist's sense of honor?"

Spittle flew from her lips as she passionately defended herself. Her small hands clenched, the well-manicured nails digging into the flesh of her palms. She felt sweat gather at her hairline, break out beneath her arms. She was no Vulcan, to deny her emotions. Jekri felt her emotions deeply, and she knew she had to convince the powerful Triumvirate of her government of her sincerity, or else Telek R'Mor's family would not die unaccompanied.

For a long, agonizing moment, the faces on the screen remained angry. Then the three exchanged glances. The Empress nodded, as if she had just had something confirmed, and resumed her seat. Jekri closed her eyes briefly and licked her lips. She tasted the salt of her fear on her tongue.

"Praetor, Proconsul, Empress, frankly, the Shepherds do not care whether Jekri Baseborn has clawed her way up through the ranks and whether she is to be plunged back down into the sewers from which she emerged," said Lhiau. Furious, Jekri whirled, but he continued speaking.

"Personally, I would just as soon work with someone else. But it matters little, in the end. What does matter"—his voice dropped to a growl and he leaned menacingly into the viewscreen—"is getting Telek R'Mor *back*. We want him. We need him—and that damned ship as well. Do you understand? If you want to keep your precious cloaks, you will do as I demand!"

Jekri pressed her lips together. In her entire life, she had never heard anyone address the Triumvirate in such insulting tones. The Proconsul, who loved his position rather more than he ought, was probably bursting a vein or two by staying silent.

"Ambassador Lhiau," said the Praetor, his reedy voice meant to be soothing, "please know that we are extremely grateful for the gift of the dark matter cloaking apparatus, and that we will do everything in our power to try—"

"No!" Lhiau had dropped all pretense of cordiality now. His face was flushed, his eyes wild. "You will not *try* anything! You will *find* Telek, *find Voyager,* and bring them to me! Or else, mark me well, Triumvirate, you will all three desperately wish you had never been born!"

He stabbed down with a forefinger and terminated the conversation. Jekri stared in open-mouthed shock. Almost immediately a red light began flashing furiously on the console—the Triumvirate, angrily trying to resume contact. Her face burned with shame and anger on behalf of her superiors.

"Who do you think you are?" she hissed between clenched teeth.

He glanced down at her contemptuously, then left without even answering.

Jekri let the red light blink for a moment while she gathered her thoughts. She had not come as far as she had in this life without trusting her instincts, and everything in her was screaming that Lhiau could not, and should not, be trusted. The cloaking technology he offered was exciting; it would advance the Romulan Empire beyond anyone's wildest dreams. But Jekri knew better than to believe that anyone, even the rulers of her Empire, could get something for nothing. And as she turned back to the angry red light to resume the abruptly terminated conversation with the Triumvirate, she wondered when Lhiau would collect payment, and just what that payment might be.

She would watch him. And wait.

Neelix was anxious to make their new guest feel at home. He had taken it upon himself to give Telek a tour of *Voyager*. There had been some concern about showing Telek too much; if, by some freak chance of fate he were to return to his own time and place, he would know a great deal about how far the Federation had come in twenty years. Such knowledge could—and certainly would—be exploited by others with less conscience than their highly principled visitor. When Neelix had mentioned that concern, Telek had looked hopeful for an instant, then relapsed into resigned sorrow.

"It is doubtful I will ever return, but should that happen, I would be more than content to have my memories of my time here erased. That is," he had added, "if Commander Tuvok would agree to a mind meld."

"It is an intimate contact," said Tuvok, "but for the higher good, if the situation arose I would agree."

Neelix had been pleased. This way, they could open their arms to the man who had sacrificed his family, and do what pathetically little they could to make him feel welcome. After setting a course that zigzagged in as unpredictable a manner as they could contrive yet still kept them heading in the general direction of the Alpha Quadrant, Telek was released into Neelix's care.

Nothing made the Talaxian morale officer happier than to please others, to see them laughing and content. He suspected it would be a long, long time, if ever, before he got that reaction out of the Romulan. Telek was unfailingly courteous, and asked many polite questions as Neelix took him all around the vessel. But there was little genuine interest. He was directed inward, grieving, and Neelix's heart ached with sympathy. He, perhaps more than anyone else aboard the ship, could understand.

At one point, taking his courage in his hands, he said gently, "You know, Dr. R'Mor, I know what it's like to lose family."

Telek favored him with a mildly amused glance. "Do you indeed? What, did you experience the loss of an elderly grandfather going to the grave at a ripe old age?"

Neelix felt as though he'd been struck. He stopped dead in his tracks, momentarily choked with fury. It was not an emotion he felt often, and even as it raced along his body, tightening his muscles and sending his heart rate soaring, he was startled at its intensity. His fists clenched, but when he spoke, he forced his voice to be calm.

"I wish that was all it had been. I lost my entire family during a war in my home system. Millions died on my planet, including the one person in the universe I was closest to—my sister, Alixia. So you see, you don't have an exclusive claim to suffering!"

By the time he'd finished, Neelix was shouting the words. Startled by his outburst, he stepped backward, realizing he had been advancing menacingly on their guest.

"I—I apologize, Dr. R'Mor. I don't know what came over me."

"No, Mr. Neelix," said Telek, "it is I who owe you an apology. War is a terrible thing, and to have lost your family all at once like that must have been dreadful. I offer you my sympathy."

The anger felt good—very good. It wasn't hard to keep it simmering as Neelix regarded the Romulan. It was even easier to hear a mocking tone of voice as Telek spoke, to imagine that the Romulan didn't believe him or, worse, was belittling him.

"I'm sure you're hungry," Neelix said, the cordial words uttered in an angry tone. "This is the mess hall—*my* domain."

The door hissed open and Neelix and Telek stepped into a room buzzing with low conversation. After Telek's revelation, Janeway had ordered the primary shift on duty, and people were eager for coffee and something to break their fasts. Neelix had earlier set out an array of cold foodstuffs to which people could help themselves. Now, with his unpleasant task of escorting the arrogant Romulan out of the way, he moved quickly to don his chef's hat and apron and prepare something hot and satisfying to the *real*, deserving members of the crew.

He felt Telek's gaze on him, but ignored it. The Romulan stood for a while, looking about hesitantly. *Good*, thought Neelix, breaking some Skelonian spotted eggs into a bowl and whisking them into a green froth with unnecessary fervor. *I hope he feels as out of place as he really is—out of place, out of time . . . !*

He'd planned to instruct Telek on the use of the replicator. He'd planned to inquire about native Romulan foods and prepare them as carefully and accurately as possible. Now, he almost hoped Telek would choke on the coffee.

Finally, Telek made his way to a seat. He folded his hands in front of him and looked lost.

"Who's that?" It was the clear, high voice of Naomi Wildman, *Voyager*'s youngest crew member. Neelix glanced down. His spirits lifted a little at the sight of his goddaughter.

"Well, good morning!" he enthused. "You're up early."

"My mom got called to duty and I got bored trying to sleep." She stood on her tiptoes and reached for a deep blue *thal* fruit. "You didn't answer my question." Her large eyes fastened on him, she crunched down on the fruit.

"Oh. He's a Romulan," said Neelix, the anger surging to the fore again. "It's a long story."

Naomi swallowed, wiped at her mouth, took another bite, and regarded the Romulan with a serious gaze suited to one much older.

"He looks lonely. Maybe he'd like to play with Flotter and me in the holodeck this afternoon. I'll go ask him."

"Naomi, I don't think—" Neelix called, but the little girl, her long red-blond hair swinging down her back, had already clambered into the chair opposite Telek R'Mor.

"Hi, I'm Naomi Wildman," said the child, offering a sticky, juice-stained hand.

Cautiously, Telek accepted her hand and shook it politely. "Greetings, Naomi Wildman. I did not expect to see a child aboard a Federation starship."

"My mom was pregnant with me when we got pulled into the Delta Quadrant," Naomi explained. "She didn't expect to be gone so long."

"I see," Telek replied. He hesitated, then said softly, "It must be a great comfort to your mother to have you here with her so far away from home."

"I guess so. Sometimes Mom says she really misses my dad."

"But you," said Telek, sorrow creeping into his voice, "you have never seen your father, and thus cannot miss him."

"I'm a little nervous about meeting him," Naomi confided. "But Mom says I'll like him a lot."

"I am sure you will, child," Telek said.

Naomi studied him, legs swinging as she continued to chew the fruit. "Are you a daddy?"

Telek stood abruptly. "I think perhaps your captain and I should talk again. I must go. It was pleasant meeting you, Naomi Wildman."

Her face fell. "But . . . aren't you hungry? I can tell you what the best things to eat are, if you're not used to eating our food. The replicator can make chocolate cake, and ice cream, and *ba-ti-kaa'*, and—"

"That is thoughtful of you. Perhaps another time." He nodded, rose, and exited quickly.

Neelix watched him leave, then glanced back at Naomi. The little girl followed Telek with her gaze, and when the door had closed behind the Romulan, she silently, deliberately placed her half-eaten fruit on the table and clasped her hands in her lap. She stared down at her fingers. The look on her face broke Neelix's heart.

How cruel that Telek R'Mor was.

Neelix's spotted hand reached out and closed on a knife. He was proud of the tools of his trade. All his knives were replicas of the finest chef's knives of the known galaxy. Part of his evening ritual, before he closed the mess for the night, was to carefully clean and sharpen each blade. They would be ready for him in the morning, ready to slice fruits and vegetables for juicing so that the crew would feast on only the finest, freshest foods.

This particular knife had a ten-centimeter blade.

He had sliced only a few fruits with it that morning. The Romulan had taken up all his time. Carefully, Neelix tested it with his thumb. Plenty sharp to do the next task.

Moving quickly and purposefully, Neelix slipped from behind the counter and strode out of the mess hall.

Telek hadn't gone far. Contrary to what he had told Naomi, he seemed in no hurry to meet with anyone. He'd lied to her, then. He walked slowly down the corridor, head bowed, hands clasped behind his back. He seemed unaware of Neelix, who moved quickly and quietly to close the distance between them.

He belittled Alixia's murder. He hurt Naomi. He's a Romulan, a traitor to his people, a traitor from a race of traitors—

He lifted the knife.

Neelix knew he hadn't made a sound, but something alerted the Romulan. Some unnatural sixth sense, perhaps. Telek's head jerked upward and he whirled around, bringing his hand up to close hard on Neelix's wrist.

Neelix grunted. He was stronger than he looked, and he was fueled by a hatred that seemed to have no beginning and no end. He managed to keep his grip on the knife despite the crushing pressure that Telek's long fingers exerted.

Just a little lower—his chest is unprotected—finally put an end to him—

Neelix heard running footsteps and the warbling

chirp of a combadge being activated. "This is Naomi Wildman," came a high voice treble with fear. "Please, somebody, stop him, he's trying to hurt Mr. R'Mor!"

Startled, Neelix turned around, and in that instant Telek overcame him. Strong fingers closed around his throat and began to tighten. The knife fell from Neelix's hand as he instinctively tried to pry the throttling fingers away from his neck. The carpeted floor of the corridor rushed up to meet him and he knew no more.

"Are you absolutely certain it was Neelix?" Janeway couldn't believe what she was hearing and repeated the question for the second or third time.

"Yes," said Telek. He, Janeway, and Tuvok stood at the foot of the Talaxian's bed in sickbay. The Doctor moved quickly and efficiently. "Naomi can stand witness for me."

Janeway glanced at the girl, presently seated on another bed. The child clung to her mother. She was trying very hard not to cry, but clearly she was quite upset.

Yielding to impulse, Janeway went to the Wildmans. "Samantha, I'm sure there's an explanation for all this," she said gently.

The blonde ensign favored her with a quick, angry glance. "He's her godfather. And look what he's done to her! My poor baby . . . ."

Janeway frowned. Samantha Wildman and Neelix were very close. It wasn't like the ensign to assume that the blame was entirely Neelix's. After all, there was a stranger on board. Turning back to that stranger, Janeway planted her hands on her hips.

"Naomi has confirmed that the two of you were fighting in the hallway, and that Neelix had a knife. She also confirmed that you left the mess hall first and he followed. But I know my crewman, Dr. R'Mor. Of everyone on the ship, with the exception of little Naomi herself, Neelix is the last person I'd expect to initiate an attack on a stranger."

Telek's expression revealed nothing. "Perhaps he has cause to hate my people."

"He's a Delta Quadrant native, dammit! He's never even heard of the Romulans before! How the hell is he going to develop a grudge against—"

"Captain! Stop shouting!" The Doctor's voice was strident, as angry as Janeway's own.

Janeway's temple throbbed and she rubbed it. Her heart was beating rapidly and her face was hot with the rising anger she had so abruptly quelled. The Doctor, too, looked furious, more so than her sharp words would have warranted. His dark eyes snapped and veins bulged in his neck.

"Sorry, Doctor. Seems like this stress is beginning to affect all of us, even you."

Telek stepped forward and grasped Janeway's arm, hard. "What did you say?"

Tuvok reached for his phaser, but Janeway didn't need his help.

"Let go of me." She said the words coldly and clearly. At once, the Romulan released her.

"Forgive me, Captain, but I fear— You spoke of

stress affecting even the Doctor, a being who is merely a hologram."

"You'd drop that 'merely' if Mr. Neelix had managed to stick that knife in you," muttered the Doctor as he regarded the medical tricorder's readings.

Telek ignored the gibe. "Doctor, what is Neelix's condition?"

"I'm not entirely certain," said the Doctor. "His white blood cell count is abnormally high. The endocrine system is releasing a flood of hormones, as if he's in an extremely stressful, perhaps even dangerous situation. But he's unconscious. He's not even dreaming. The hypothalamus is unusually active as well. There are contusions on the throat that, coincidentally enough, correspond to the exact shape of a certain Romulan's fingers, but those can be healed rapidly. He should be coming around shortly."

The Doctor scowled. "Captain, I'd like to run some tests on him. There may be an infection of some sort that is targeting the upper brain stem, or an injury we weren't aware of."

"An infection," Telek repeated, as if to himself. "Yes, those words will do as well as any." More loudly, he said, "Captain, Doctor, I have an unusual request regarding Neelix, especially given the circumstances. I wish to work with the Doctor while he conducts his tests, and I also need to have access to your computer system. And I will require a crew member to assist me, someone who has a wide variety of experiences . . . and an open mind."

"Captain," Tuvok said. "Dr. R'Mor has been involved in an incident involving potential homicide. I do not think it wise to grant him any access to either Mr. Neelix or *Voyager*'s databanks until the situation is resolved."

Janeway rubbed her throbbing temple. "What is it you hope to find, Telek?"

"I cannot say at this juncture. It is a merely a hypothesis—one I hope is very wrong. Please, Captain. You may have a guard with a phaser to my head at all times if that would satisfy your Vulcan guard dog." His eyebrows lifted and he looked immediately chagrined, as if the sneering words had popped out of his mouth without his volition.

"My so-called Vulcan guard dog will indeed be with you at all times," Janeway said, "but since you seem to have a theory as to what's happening with Mr. Neelix, I'm going to grant your request."

"Captain!" The Doctor seemed livid. "Telek R'Mor is responsible for putting Mr. Neelix here in the first place! I hardly think it appropriate to have him poking around sickbay, getting in the way at the very least."

"He's responsible for the bruises to Neelix's throat," Janeway agreed. "But what about the hyperactive immune system you mentioned, Doctor? The flood of hormones? Did Telek do that too?"

The Doctor fell silent. Janeway turned again to Telek. "I can meet half your request regarding a crewman. Seven of Nine has the widest variety of experiences and knowledge on this ship, but I don't know how open her mind is."

"Thank you, Captain. I will report to you as soon as I know anything."

"Yes," said the Doctor forcefully. *"We* will."

Romulan. Aggressive, intelligent species bent on galactic domination. An offshoot of the Vulcan race, the Romulans possess the same powerful physical strength but do not have the emotional control exhibited by Vulcans. Their biological and technological distinctiveness was added to our—

Seven shook her head, as if she could physically dislodge the disconcerting thoughts. She had been on *Voyager* for over two years now. She was more human than Borg. And yet, every time she met a new race, she immediately lapsed into the old, Borg way of cataloging them.

She did not like it.

Seven forced herself to return her attention to the task at hand. Long fingers, some formed of flesh and some of metal, flew over the controls as she broke down the sample of Neelix's brain tissue into its various components and entered the formula Telek had requested.

She saw nothing unusual and was about to move on when the shadow of the Romulan fell across the console.

"Wait a moment," said Telek. "If I may . . . ."

Without waiting for an answer, he stepped forward and adjusted the controls. He tapped in a second formula, frowned, entered a third. Seven raised an eyebrow in admiration. This scientist knew what he was doing. In fact, he knew more than she did. The numbers meant nothing to her, the formula was a jumble. She was about to open her mouth to request that he explain what he was doing when Telek stiffened.

"You have found something?" she asked.

At once, the Doctor was at their side, peering over Telek's shoulder. "What is it?"

Telek's deft fingers flew again over the controls. An image appeared, barely visible. "Computer," he instructed, "enlarge image."

Seven realized she was looking at a single cell. Genetic material floated in the watery cytoplasm, enclosed within the plasma membrane. So much she was familiar with.

"Computer, enlarge grid C-four." At once, the computer focused on and enlarged the requested grid. "Again."

Seven frowned. A small black dot floated freely in the cytoplasm. "That is unlike anything I have ever seen," she said.

"That," said Telek heavily, "is because it *is* something you have never seen. Computer, calculate estimated amount of gravity on this vessel. Cross-reference with known amount of matter present."

Seven and the Doctor exchanged puzzled glances. What was Telek doing? How did this absurd exercise relate to Neelix's condition, or the strange black dot floating about in one of his cells?

"Calculation complete," said the computer in its cool, crisp, female voice. "There is a discrepancy of .000000173 grams."

"Lighter or heavier?"

"Heavier."

"Doctor R'Mor," began the Doctor, "we are allegedly working *with* you in solving this conundrum. Perhaps you'd care to enlighten us?"

"A moment, Doctor," Telek replied absently. "Seven of Nine, can you run this calculation on *Voyager*'s— what were they? The gel packs we were discussing?"

"Bio-neural gel packs," Seven replied.

"Yes, of course. Can you run the calculation on the bio-neural gel packs and the structure of the ship itself, if you would."

Seven let the accomplishment of the task be the answer. Unaccustomed to human reaction as she still was, she felt the prickling of hair along her body as a primal chill raced through her when she saw what her calculations yielded. In both the physical structure of the vessel and in the bio-neural gel packs, there was clear evidence of the same mysterious black dots that they had discovered in Neelix's body.

"Behold one of the greatest mysteries of science of this or any era," said Telek, his voice filled with both harshness and wonder.

"What is this we are seeing?" demanded the Doctor.

Telek looked him square in the eye. "Something that has until recently never revealed itself to mortal eyes. You have the dubious pleasure of looking upon an individual particle of dark matter itself."

CHAPTER
4

JANEWAY STARED AT THE BLACK SPOT ON NEELIX'S brain cell. A slow, hot anger rose in her.

"Whatever you may think of us, Telek, surely you know we're not fools. Dark matter isn't the mystery it was to us a few hundred years ago. We've even piloted *Voyager* through a dark-matter nebula, and the only threat we encountered was from the beings who lived inside it. The stuff may not be ordinary matter, but it is harmless, and it certainly doesn't go around manifesting in peoples' brain cells and turning them homicidal. I know what dark matter is, and I know that this isn't it!"

She whirled on Telek. "What are you trying to do, Telek? What is this?"

Telek's control was admirable. He met Janeway's accusing stare evenly. "I will forgive your overreaction, Captain, because I know what is transpiring and that you are not yourself. You are right. Normally, dark matter is indeed quite harmless. You have never encountered dark matter in its natural state, or, to be more specific, you have never been aware of doing so."

"Stop talking in riddles," snapped Janeway.

"You know as well as I that dark matter is visible only when it clusters together in a nebula," Telek replied, his voice rising. "You Federation types, you brag about your scientific knowledge, as if no one could possibly know more than you. Well, I do, Captain. Have you not noticed that a dark-matter nebula manifests only where there is a disturbance in subspace? Do you think that a mere coincidence?"

Surprised, Janeway straightened. "Go on."

"We speak of the matter that makes up at least ninety percent of the universe, perhaps even more. Yet the gravity of each individual particle is minute. Even the amount of dark matter present on *Voyager* now weighs less than a gram. Therefore, there must be more, much, much more, dark matter than exists in a cluster such as a dark-matter nebula. Decades of Romulan research leads me to believe that dark matter is present everywhere throughout the universe, that it passes right through our bodies on a daily basis."

"First you say that Neelix's situation is being caused by dark matter. Then you say that the stuff is harmless. Which is it, Telek?" demanded Chakotay.

Telek looked at the shiny surface of the table. "Ordinary dark matter *is* harmless. But what is inside Neelix's brain is not ordinary dark matter. I have told you the Shepherds know how to manipulate it, have given us cloaks and improved wormhole technology. I spoke earlier of the phenomenon of the dark-matter nebula, a collision of distorted subspace and natural dark matter that renders the dark matter visible."

He looked up from the table and met Janeway's eyes evenly. "Something similar occurs when dark matter enters a wormhole. A wormhole is not normal space, and the same kind of interaction happens. The dark matter is transformed. It becomes visible, just as in a dark-matter nebula."

Janeway's head hurt so badly she could barely see straight, but she took a deep, calming breath and tried to make sense of Telek's words.

"Let me see if I'm following this," said Harry Kim slowly. "I know that dark matter isn't made up of the same material as ordinary matter—what comprises suns and stars and even flesh. You're saying that because we know that dark matter makes up most of the matter of the universe—"

"Ninety percent," emphasized Telek. "Only an estimated ten percent of the universe's matter is ordinary, baryonic matter."

"Okay, okay, ninety percent," said Harry. "So there's got to be more than the occasional dark-matter nebula."

"Yes, yes," said Telek, who seemed to be impatient with Harry's step-by-step reasoning.

"So much more, in fact, that it's passing through

our bodies right this minute," the ensign continued. "And even though that's probably been happening ever since the universe was created, you're saying that the dark matter that the Shepherds have been playing with—the same dark matter that's visible when it interacts with subspace distortions—is now so dangerous it's driving Neelix crazy?"

"Yes," said Telek, "that is correct, as far as it goes. You say you have passed unharmed through a dark-matter nebula. I'm not surprised. You were probably not within the nebula for a sufficient amount of time for the mutated dark matter to lodge within you or your vessel. But for a long time now, I have been seeking you. You have been exposed to a powerful burst of dark matter as it emerges from each wormhole. Think of it, Ensign Kim—how many wormholes have opened and closed over the last few days?"

Harry looked unwell. "Hundreds."

"Yes. And all with the sole purpose of finding you and your ship. I deeply regret it, but it seems that I am indirectly responsible for your present situation."

Janeway turned to the Doctor. "You've been studying this, Doctor. What do you think? Is Telek's theory valid?"

The Doctor hesitated before replying. "My findings are preliminary, but I have enough information to worry me. Whatever these particles are, they're in the cells of every crew member and inside the ship itself and all its programs." He paused, huffed a little, and added, "Including myself."

"Do you believe this is what caused Neelix to attack Telek?" asked Chakotay.

"At this juncture, I'd say yes," the Doctor said. "There were several particles of the matter clustered together in his hypothalamus, which is the area of the brain that directs emotions. You, Captain, have several clusters in the capillaries that supply blood to your brain."

"That explains the headaches," sighed Janeway.

"To a greater or lesser extent, we are all affected," said the Doctor, glancing around at the senior staff.

"It's inside us," said Paris softly. "It's inside us *all.*" One hand reached up to his chest and scratched at his heart. His blue eyes regarded Telek with fear and hatred commingled. "And you brought it here, you son of a bitch."

"Tom!" snapped Janeway.

"Captain, how do we know he's not a Romulan spy, sent here to destroy us?" Paris leaped to his feet. The chair rolled away with the motion. "Maybe he brought this . . . this mutant dark matter here deliberately. You know Romulans, always trying to conquer the universe—"

"Ensign!" Chakotay shouted. "Sit down or I'll have you thrown in the brig! Hell, I'll throw you in there myself!"

Tom stared at the commander defiantly before finally sitting. It was clear that he was being affected by the dark matter presently in his system, but something about what he said made sense to Janeway. Paranoia rose in her, but she quelled it with an effort.

"Of course you are suspicious," said Telek. "But I imagine that by now I, too, have been . . . infected. Doctor, if you would scan me, please?"

The Doctor brought out his medical tricorder and quickly ran the instrument over the Romulan. "It's true, Captain. There is mutated dark matter present in Telek's system as well—not nearly as much as we have, but it's there."

Telek narrowed his eyes. "I have told you, Captain. It is dark matter, corrupted by being inside the wormhole."

Janeway rose and stretched, trying to distract herself from the agony in her head. She went over everything she knew about dark matter and could find no flaw in Telek's theory. No flaw, that is, except the obvious one—it hadn't been proved. Still, he was right. A dark-matter nebula never occurred separately from a subspace distortion. But what was it about subspace, or wormhole space, that turned harmless dark matter into dangerous particles?

"So. We've got dark matter—excuse me, mutated dark matter—in our bodies and in our ship. It's giving me a headache, making Tom paranoid and Neelix homicidal. What else is it going to do?"

Telek was silent. "I fear the worst. It will not get better on its own, Captain, that much I know."

"He's right," confirmed the Doctor. "Neelix's condition is worsening, not improving."

"And my headache isn't going away either," said Janeway. It was an understatement. "Now, gentlemen and ladies, the question of the hour: How do we stop it?"

All eyes turned to the Romulan. For the first time since Janeway had seen him, he looked helpless. His ignorance was written on his face, and she felt her gut clench. He had no idea what to do.

She glanced at the Doctor. "Do you have any suggestions?"

The Doctor looked thoughtful. "The dark matter is behaving much like an infectious agent. It invades the body and begins to replicate itself, interfering with normal bodily functions and causing damage to tissue throughout the body. If we continue with this metaphor of an infection or a cancer, we could try treating it in such a manner. We could attempt to remove the dark matter surgically, or else expose it to various types of radiation in the hope that—"

"No!" Telek interrupted harshly. "No, do not attempt to apply any type of radiation to this. It reacts in a completely unpredictable fashion."

"Then we're back to trying to remove it," said Janeway. "But how? We've discussed surgery, but from the look on your face, Doctor, that would appear to be tricky."

"Beam the stuff out," said Torres.

"It cannot be dematerialized," said Telek.

"Oh, come on," said Torres, exasperated, "if it's matter, it can be dematerialized."

"I repeat, dark matter is not matter as we know it," replied Telek.

Torres threw her hands up and made an exasperated noise. "So, you've shot down all our ideas. What's yours?"

He did not reply for a moment, then said softly, "We need to find the Shepherds."

"I hate the Shepherds," Subcommander Verrak muttered to his superior officer as they worked, side by side, trying to decipher Telek R'Mor's encrypted notes.

"You are not alone," Jekri whispered back. Her face was still hot at the memory of the tongue-lashing she'd received from the Triumvirate. A reprimand was never a pleasant thing, but the three had vented their anger upon Jekri for things Lhiau had done. The unjustness of it rankled. She would be more than happy when victory in the Alpha Quadrant was assured and the Shepherds had gone back to wherever it was they'd crawled from.

"The Triumvirate was wrong to address you so," said Verrak, growing slightly more bold. "It is Lhiau's arrogance that has upset them."

"The Triumvirate is never wrong," said Jekri, "even when it is misguided. Do you understand?" She shot him a look from silver eyes.

Swallowing, the young man nodded. Jekri turned back to her work, feeling Verrak's gaze linger on her face for a moment longer.

She knew her subcommander was beginning to develop feelings for her, and that both of them realized how inappropriate such feelings were. Mates and children were fine for simple folk like scientists and artists. Politicians—especially those whose work required an intimate acquaintance with the darker side of life—needed to have more control. It had been a long time since Jekri had permitted herself the indulgence of a coupling, and she had never been able or willing to make herself vulnerable to something as dangerous as love.

Verrak was a loyal and hardworking member of her immediate circle. That he was sometimes comforting to be around and definitely attractive was irrelevant. He, however, did not seem to have as much control over himself as she did, and she worried that his emotions might cause him to make a mistake. And mistakes were something Jekri would not tolerate, not at this juncture.

"The Shepherds have already given us sufficient apparatuses to cloak thirteen warbirds," Verrak continued, keeping his eyes on the screen as he spoke. "We know they can operate when the ships are at warp. There are those who think the Triumvirate may be missing a rare opportunity, that we should launch our attack on the Federation now, before these Shepherds have a chance to change their minds."

Apprehension spurted through Jekri. She glanced up. There was no sign of Lhiau, but that didn't reassure her. How were they to be sure that these Shepherds couldn't make themselves invisible, or listen from a great distance? There was so much about the Shepherds they didn't know, and Jekri even doubted what Lhiau had chosen to tell them.

"We made a bargain with them," she said, her

whisper sharp and angry. "We must uphold our end. We must get *Voyager* and Telek R'Mor back before we can implement our plan to attack the Federation. Besides, *Voyager* is necessary to our success."

Heedless of who saw, Verrak turned and regarded her directly. "Is it? Thirteen undetectable warbirds, which could fire without once dropping their cloaks, could take the Federation by the throat! And what do we owe to *bikk'raa* like the Shepherds? Lhiau uses every opportunity to insult the Empress, the Senate, the Praetor—even you, Chairman. Even you and the Tal Shiar."

His voice was tinged with wonder, and it was balm to Jekri's spirit. She smarted under the stinging insults that dripped so casually from Lhiau's mouth, and it was beyond her comprehension how so esteemed a personage as the Empress, indeed the whole Triumvirate, could continue to tolerate such affronts.

But the Shepherds offered quadrant, if not galactic, domination, and that was a tidbit worth shutting one's mouth to take.

"I cannot bear it that he says such things to you," Verrak continued, his voice warm and husky. His fists clenched and his throat worked, and Jekri's breath caught for the briefest of moments in her throat at this revelation.

At once, she quelled it. Verrak could get them all killed. She rose, standing over him as he remained seated, and backhanded his face as hard as she could.

"Looking at all these confusing codes must have

addled my brain," she said. "I thought I heard words that could be construed as treason from you, Sub-commander. But surely I was mistaken."

The green imprint of her blow stood out on his cheek. Verrak's face was impassive, the glow of concern—or something deeper—gone. "No treason, Chairman. I am a loyal servant of the Empire."

"As I know you to be," she said, softening her rebuke slightly. "I will send someone with a fresher pair of eyes to work with you." Without another word, she strode from the tiny room into another tiny room. But here in Telek's quarters, at least, she was alone.

Her body thrummed with emotions—anger, fear, a touch, perhaps, of desire if she should care to name it so. Sighing heavily, Jekri dropped down on the bed and removed her boots.

Verrak's words—all of them—disturbed her deeply. He was right. They could probably take on the Federation with their present number of dark matter–cloaked vessels. But the Triumvirate, true to their Romulan heritage, wanted to wait until there was no risk at all. They didn't want to fight the Federation. They wanted to sweep in with a victory so overwhelming that the round-ears wouldn't even know what had hit them.

And, had the Shepherd displayed any hint of good breeding or courtesy, Jekri probably would have agreed wholeheartedly with this plan of action. But Lhiau was unbearable. She did not trust him, and she didn't see how the Triumvirate could.

She placed her hands behind her head as she lay on the bed and stared at the ceiling. From the moment she joined the Tal Shiar after executing an unauthorized—but highly desired—assassination for them, Jekri had ceased to accept insults. The mantle of the intelligence service shielded her almost completely, and on the rare occasions when someone had dared show her anything but the utmost respect it had been a matter of hours before she had been able to find some charge upon which to arrest him. She was sorry that, as she moved with blazing swiftness up the ranks of the Tal Shiar, her higher positions took her away from administering interrogations personally.

She turned her head and regarded the holophoto of Telek's wife and child that the scientist had placed beside his bed. Jekri had never bothered to learn their names. The woman was quite lovely, and the child appealing. She realized that, in all the chaos, she had forgotten to give the order for their torture and execution. It was just one more thing on a long, long list of things to do. A chairman's work was never done.

Sighing, she closed her eyes. She'd get to the order after a quick nap. Even behind closed lids, she saw the dancing images of Telek R'Mor's encrypted formulas.

CHAPTER

5

"ATTENTION, ALL CREW. THIS IS CAPTAIN JANEWAY. We will shortly be going to Yellow Alert, and we will maintain that alert for some time. Please report to your duty stations for a briefing from your section's senior officer for more details. If you are not presently on duty, stay in your quarters until further notice. For the time being, I am placing the holodeck and all other nonessential operations of this vessel off limits. Janeway out."

Naomi, nearly breaking into a run to keep up with the brisk pace of her mother, let out a whimper. "The holodeck? Why? What's happening, Mama?"

Naomi could be quiet when she chose, and had sharp ears. She had heard and seen enough to know that something serious was going on. She'd caught a few words that had scared her: "possible malfunction . . . infection . . . unpredictable."

"Nothing you need to worry about," her mother replied brusquely. She was almost marching the girl toward their quarters, and Naomi's heart sank. She did not want to spend several hours alone in her quarters, not when all this, whatever it was, was going on.

"Why can't I use the holodeck?"

"For God's sake, stop whining!" Samantha shook Naomi's arm angrily. Naomi shrank back a little, surprised at the outburst. "A few hundred years ago, little girls had no holodecks or even toys like Flotter, you know. They had to make do with dolls made of paper and wood and use their imaginations."

Naomi laughed at the term, and her mother's face darkened with anger. "Do whatever you want, Naomi, just don't come bothering me, all right?"

Abruptly, Samantha Wildman turned and stalked off down the corridor. Naomi, huge-eyed, stared after her.

Something bad was going on.

Well. She'd just have to make do.

Two of Four, Primary Adjunct to Seven of Nine, strode into her regeneration chamber in the cargo bay. Her Secondary, Flotter, accompanied her.

Two of Four stood tall and straight, her long red hair cascading over her shoulders, as she coolly surveyed this part of the ship that was hers and hers alone. Things could be dangerous, even here on Assignment *Voyager,* where she fit smoothly into her collective as a unique crew member. Common sense told her that it was better to have Flotter keep an eye out for anything unto—unto—

Naomi frowned. What was the word the Doctor had used the other day? Untoward, that was it.

Flotter would keep an eye out for anything untoward. "Secondary," said Two of Four in a cool, calm voice, "it is time for me to regenerate. It is a stage in which I am quite vulnerable. I entrust you with the duty of protecting me from any unto—untoward incidents."

She propped the blue doll up against a pile of storage bins and arranged its floppy blue limbs into as fierce a position as she could manage. For a moment, Two of Four—her mother was One, her absent father Three, and her beloved godfather Neelix Four—gazed at the toy, and knew that it was just a toy.

Her chest ached suddenly. No, no time for that. Seven of Nine would not have approved of such dangerous vulnerability, of such a waste of energy and time. Two of Four straightened and stepped into the cut-paper "regeneration chamber" she'd cobbled together. Things were much more fun on the holodeck, where the details were all but perfect. She was doing what her mother had told her children had done hundreds of years ago—making do with what she had and using her—

Naomi frowned. It was getting harder and harder for her to remember things for some reason. Imagination. That was the term her mother had used before she had left so abruptly.

The smile faded from Naomi's face. It was all

well and good to playact at being Seven of Nine in the regeneration chamber when Neelix was whistling in his kitchen and everyone was happily working at their posts. But now her mother was ignoring her, Seven of Nine was far too busy and had forbade her entrance into Astrometrics, and Uncle Neelix—

She sank down in her small shelter of boxes and colored paper and pulled Flotter down from his sentry post. Naomi edged as far back as she could. She felt safe and cradled here, in a cozy little spot she'd made for herself in the midst of a bustling starship.

Uncle Neelix. He'd tried to kill that nice Romulan, and despite their attempts to shield her, Naomi had heard what they'd said: "Getting worse, not better . . . might not survive."

Suddenly she hugged Flotter close. Naomi's small chest hitched and she started to cry. She was scared, so scared, and nobody was willing even to talk to her. The game was no longer fun, and she stained the doll's soft blue fabric with hot tears of loneliness and fear.

It had been a long and draining day. Janeway had been up now for over twenty hours straight. It was only when she'd begun nodding off while assisting Telek R'Mor and Seven of Nine that she realized she was becoming more of a hindrance to their quest than a help.

She began getting ready for bed and went over the events of the day in her mind. Telek's revelations had stunned them all, but at least they provided some kind of answer for what was going on aboard the ship. Neelix's attempt at murder had shocked Janeway more than she liked to admit. Such a gentle, benevolent soul. So hard to believe he would resort to violence.

Dark matter inside them. She paused in brushing her short, auburn hair and met her own eyes in the mirror. Janeway examined her reflection, as if she could see the alien matter inside her body if she looked hard enough. Unconsciously she raised a hand to touch her face, then deliberately lowered it and continued with her preparation for sleep.

The uproar that had greeted Telek's suggestion that they contact the Shepherds had been almost overwhelming. At first glance, such an idea seemed foolish at best, dangerous at worst. After all, if Telek was to be believed, weren't the Shepherds the ones who had done this in the first place? But Telek's argument had been convincing.

"Lhiau has slipped a time or two," Telek had said. "He has alluded to others who disagreed with him, and the very name he has adopted to describe his people seems contrary to his actions. What does a shepherd do? He takes care of animals. How could one destroy the flock he was sent to tend and still truly be a shepherd? No, Captain, there are other Shepherds than Lhiau, I would stake my life on it. And even if there are not, it is my opinion that the risk is worth taking. There is no alternative."

No alternative. That was a statement that had never sat particularly well with Janeway. There were always alternatives, if one looked hard enough. So she'd had the Doctor run some tests, had B'Elanna reconfigure the damned sensors, and sat down with Telek and Seven to plot out a search for alien beings who might or might not be inclined to help them.

"I'd almost welcome a visit from Q at this point," she muttered as she patted her face dry. Glancing around, although there was no one else present— yet—she added, "I said almost."

Janeway remained alone in her quarters, and for that small favor she was grateful.

Her head was killing her. After realizing what they were dealing with, the Doctor had stopped all attempts at treating her. "You'll just have to live with the pain," he'd told her. "I'll keep monitoring you to make sure it doesn't get to a dangerous point."

"Thank you," Janeway had replied dryly.

Her neck and shoulders were tense as well. She supposed she shouldn't be surprised. A warm room often helped to relax her as she slept, so she asked the computer to turn up the heat a few degrees. Janeway took a washcloth, dunked it in cold water, wrung it out, and pressed the cold cloth to her forehead. It was an old-fashioned trick from the days when headaches were more common than now, and she'd found that it even worked a little.

"Lights," she called in a weary voice as she sank down on her bed. The room went dark, save for the constant, faint illumination of the stars.

She pulled the blankets up to her chin, took a deep

breath, and surrendered to the warm comfort of her bed. The warmth

—heat—

enveloped her and sleep, for once, came easily.

Janeway wiped a hand across her dripping forehead. For not the first time, she wondered why she kept her hair long. Short hair certainly would have helped right now. At least it was bound in a neat bun on the back of her head. She breathed through the specially treated cloth the doctor had ordered they all wear and was grateful for it. The air was thick and heavy and filled with ash.

The planet had no humanoid inhabitants, and as far as they could determine, no sentient life-forms at all. The study of the volcano and how it affected the rain forest environment could therefore be undertaken without concern for the Prime Directive. The air was filled with the cries of animals, though, and as a bright scarlet-and-purple winged creature flew overhead in a panic, Janeway felt for the beasts.

Beside her crouched the rest of her away team, Ensign Pakriti and Lieutenant Yvonne Harper. She could hear their labored breathing—or was it just her own that she heard?

Janeway tossed in her bed, aware that she was dreaming, yet unable to stop it. She did not want to see this, not again, not able to do anything to stop it, to change her decision . . . .

She studied her tricorder. "If my calculations are correct, there won't be another seismic tremor for another twenty-two point seven minutes." She glanced at her crew. "That's enough time for us to split up and get three different readings on that unusual radiation at the center. Harper, you go there. Pakriti, head for that area over there. I'll go right for the heart of the thing."

They adjusted their tricorders to emit a warning sound halfway though their allotted time and agreed to reconvene at this spot.

Then they took off running.

The earth tremor hit six minutes later.

Janeway was thrown hard, but the only debris that showered her prone form was dust and small chunks of earth. Her protective mouth covering was torn away and she coughed, her lungs seared from the smoke.

She heard a faint cry of pain. No, two—one closer than the other. She stumbled to her feet and went to the closer one. Pakriti, his elongated features twisted in pain, was trapped beneath a fallen tree. Grunting, Janeway pushed and struggled, and finally managed to shove the tree off the wounded Kiltarian. A human would have been killed, but Pakriti's stronger bone structure had saved him. Even so, he was injured.

"Come on," Janeway said. She pulled Pakriti's arm around her shoulders and walked with him to the cleared area. The radiation closer to the volcano interfered with the transporter. "Lock on to Pakriti's signal and beam him to sickbay," she said, then headed back out in search of Harper.

A second tremor shook the earth. A huge gap opened up almost beneath Janeway's feet and she hurled herself clear. She felt as if she were riding a wild beast. Nothing was certain, when you couldn't even trust the earth you walked on.

Her tricorder had fallen into the chasm that had opened a scant meter from her left arm. Janeway got to her feet and grimly went in the direction from which she had last heard Harper's cry.

She found the ensign a few moments later. Yvonne was unconscious, and for a bad few seconds Janeway thought the younger woman was dead. Debris and rocks covered almost all her body. Grimly Janeway began to remove the pile, stone by stone.

She'd gotten the girl safely back to the *Billings*. She herself had to be treated for radiation poisoning, smoke inhalation, and minor lacerations. The doctor predicted a full recovery for all three members of the away team and sent Janeway to her quarters for a day or two.

Let it end here, the sleeping Janeway pleaded with her subconscious. *I know what happened. I don't want to live it again. Please.*

"Commander."

The voice was soft and feminine, and Janeway stirred, frowning. That wasn't her title. She was captain now, captain of the *U.S.S. Voyager.*

"Commander Janeway."

The soft voice had an edge to it. Janeway trembled on the verge of recognition and opened her eyes.

She was standing in her quarters on the *U.S.S. Billings.* Nothing unusual about that. Standing just outside the door was Ensign Yvonne Harper. Janeway was surprised to see the young woman.

"Yvonne, please come in. What can I do for you?"

Harper didn't move. She just stared at Janeway, her brown eyes dark and unreadable. "I don't want to come in. And there's nothing you can do for me. You've already done enough."

"I don't understand."

"My legs," Harper said softly. "They're artificial."

Janeway had known that Harper's legs would have to be removed. They had been far too badly crushed, and too long a time had passed to repair them. She had been sorry for the woman, but she knew several Federation veterans who had artificial limbs. Some of them bragged that they were better than the real ones. Most could barely tell the difference when they thought about it at all. She opened her mouth, but Harper pressed on.

"And my face. It's all reconstructed. My *face* . . . ." Her voice trailed off and one hand went to her nose, her cheek. Janeway couldn't tell the difference. Harper was an uncommonly lovely woman. Janeway had always felt she herself was attractive enough, but knew she was no striking beauty. She'd never wanted to be.

"You're so pretty, Yvonne," she said softly. "No one could tell that—"

"Shut up!" Janeway stared. Yvonne was getting worked up now. "That's not the worst of it. Do you know what happened to me out there? Do you know? Did they tell you, tell everyone? You left me out there, Kathryn, you left me out there buried beneath rocks and stones while you spent all your time with Pakriti. And do you know what that did to me?"

A sob shook her and she replied in a thick voice, *"I lost my child!"*

Janeway felt as if she'd been slapped in the face. She didn't even know Yvonne was pregnant. The lieutenant would never have been sent on such a dangerous mission if Janeway had known. Yvonne had been married only a few months and had never requested special assignments. How was anyone to know?

"Oh, Yvonne," Janeway said, compassion flooding her. She took a step toward the woman, reached out her arms to embrace her. "I'm so sorry, I—"

Yvonne twisted to evade Janeway's touch. Her eyes weren't dull and empty anymore. They were filled with hate. "I'm leaving. I'm leaving Starfleet, and I'm probably leaving James too. I can't be around . . . I can't . . . Oh, God, Kathryn, didn't you hear me calling? *Why didn't you come for me?"*

The answers were right out of Starfleet regulations. They sat, unsaid, on Janeway's lips. Pakriti was closer. You went to help the one that was closest, that's how it was done. She didn't know Harper was the more gravely injured, certainly didn't know that Harper carried a new life within her that had been lost because of the injury.

Later, Janeway would hear, through whispered rumors, that Harper had gone into a mental hospital after an attempted suicide. It might have been rumor, it might not. She could never bring herself to check and find out.

"Why didn't you come for me?" Yvonne's wrists were bloody. "Why did you leave me?" Now her

face was burned with a self-inflicted phaser blast.
"Why?" A thin line ran across her throat from the
rope she'd hanged herself with. "Your decision. Your
decision."

"No!" Captain Kathryn Janeway bolted upright.
She had clutched the sheets in a death grip and her
fingers ached. Tears were wet on her face, and her
throat hurt from the scream of protest. She was covered in sweat. There was no volcano, no *Billings*, no
Pakriti, no Yvonne Harper, dead or alive. Only a hot,
stifling room and the cold, wet sensation of the
washcloth she'd dampened and pressed to her forehead to ease away a headache caused by mutated
dark matter rampaging through her system.

Shaking, she got to her feet. "Lights," she called,
in a rasping voice. With hands that trembled, she
splashed water on her face and, puffy-eyed, gazed at
her haunted expression in the mirror.

Janeway had dealt with this particular memory before. She had locked it away in a corner of her mind
for many years. She'd spent many hours examining
her decision and was at peace with it. She could
have done nothing else. She didn't know how badly
Yvonne had been injured, or that she was pregnant.
She knew in her heart that she would do the same
thing again. Janeway had welcomed the lesson it had
taught her, if not the bitterness that went with it.

Except now—

Now, the dark matter that had lodged inside her
was stimulating this, one of the worst memories of
her life. It was putting her through it again, and

again, and *again*. Forcing her to relive it, make the same choice over and over, never learning, never finding peace, only the racking grief, the torment, the guilt, and the simple stark horror of what had happened. There was no lesson here, no good that would come out of this agonizing replay—only pain.

She looked ten years older. As Janeway met her eyes in the reflection, she said softly, with deeply felt emotion, "Dammit. Dammit all to hell."

"Verrak to Chairman Kaleh."

Verrak's smooth voice jolted Jekri out of a troubled, fitful doze. She had not intended to fall asleep in Telek R'Mor's bed, but she was more exhausted than she had thought. She came immediately awake, hand on her disruptor.

"Jekri here. What is it, Subcommander?"

"I think you'll want to see this."

Unbidden, a smile crept across Jekri's face. "You've cracked the code."

"Excellent," came a voice from a shadowed corner. Jekri leaped to her feet, disruptor drawn. Lhiau stepped forward—how had he gotten in here?—and nodded. "It certainly took you long enough."

"I didn't notice any Shepherds offering to lend their skills," she shot back, keeping her voice level. Lip curling in disgust, she sheathed her disruptor with exaggerated movements, showing this alien intruder just how little she feared him.

"That's not our job," he replied. "Let us go and

see what your slow but diligent subcommander has found out."

It turned out that Verrak and his team had found a key that totally shattered the encryption system. Telek R'Mor, fine scientist though he inarguably was, was not trained in the techniques of espionage. Any junior member of the Tal Shiar would have known to have at least a triple encryption system, if not a quadruple. But, though R'Mor's first layer of encryption had been sufficiently imaginative to thwart Jekri's codebreakers for several hours, once it had been cracked, there was nothing else to decipher. It was all there, laid bare to their hungry gazes—all the information they could possibly require.

"Fool," said Jekri under her breath, addressing the absent Telek. "We'll find you soon enough."

"I certainly do hope so," said Lhiau. "Your incompetence has squandered too much precious time already."

Jekri knew she needed to bite her tongue. Seated at the console, Verrak tensed, and she laid a warning hand on his shoulder. His muscles were knotted with anger, but beneath her small hand, she felt him force himself to relax. Yes, this was best. Still, she sympathized with her subcommander's obvious desire to throttle the insolent ambassador. She sympathized a great deal. Instead, with an effort, she triumphed over her gut emotions and leaned forward to see the screen.

"Telek has combined his personal thoughts with his notes," she said, her gray gaze flickering over the words. "Why, he doesn't seem to have approved of you, Ambassador. I cannot imagine why."

Lhiau pursed his red, full lips and said nothing.

"There seems to be nothing to indicate that he planned to defect," said Verrak. "Perhaps he didn't."

Jekri turned her head sharply to gaze at Verrak. "I saw him materialize on the bridge of the starship, as did you."

To his credit, Verrak didn't immediately back down in the face of his superior's rising anger. It was one of the reasons Jekri had kept him on as her sub-commander. When he thought he was right, Verrak could hold his own against anyone, even her.

"The Federation captain could have kidnapped him," Verrak pointed out. "He would be valuable to them."

Jekri didn't change her expression, but she was startled. Such a tactic had never occurred to her, but it should have. These Shepherds had managed to so distract her that she was not thinking as clearly as the chairman of the Tal Shiar ought. The revelation was unsettling.

"That is a discussion to be held when we have Telek R'Mor safely in custody," she said properly. "I am not an unfair person. R'Mor will have his Right of Statement, and perhaps he can convince me of his innocence. But for the moment, let us concentrate on his notes."

"Yes, if you don't mind." Lhiau again.

Jekri ignored him. "Can we open the worm-holes?"

"Yes," said Verrak. "We can plot and maintain their size as well. The formula is ours."

Jekri straightened and folded her arms across her breasts, thinking. "He knows our tactics," she mused. "He will alert the Federation vessel to them. By now, they know all our plans."

"Unless he is no—"

"Even if he was abducted against his will, Verrak, he will have told them our plans. His goal in contacting the Federation ship in the first place was to warn them, so they wouldn't pollute the true timeline."

This last, she uttered in a sneering tone. Jekri Kaleh was not one to believe in immutable destinies. Timelines depended on vagaries of fate. And if she could twist fate into the shape she wanted, force it to obey her considerable will, then so much the better. For the Little Dagger, there was no such thing as a "true timeline."

"We must therefore do something that he does not expect. Fortunately"—and here she stole a sidelong glance at Lhiau—"I am not in the habit of revealing everything to everyone. Verrak, implement Option Beta." She leaned forward, reading Telek's notes. "It is time to cast the net and catch our elusive fish."

CHAPTER
6

CHAKOTAY COULDN'T SLEEP. HE TRIED READING, PER-
forming some gentle stretches, sipping a cup of
herbal tea. Nothing worked. His mind was humming
along at the speed of the ship, but far less unobtru-
sively.

He knew he needed sleep. The strain and the dark
matter infesting his body were taking a toll. His pa-
tience was terribly thin, and his temper short and
rough. Sleep would help. That was when the body
healed itself, fought the dark-matter interlopers.

Finally, he sighed heavily and rose. "Lights, soft,"
he told the computer. Obligingly, the lights went on,
casting just enough illumination for him to see but
not enough to make him wince from the brightness.
Padding over to his dresser, he opened a drawer and
withdrew his medicine bundle.

For a long moment, he simply held it, feeling its familiar, comforting weight in his hands. Chakotay wondered if he was doing the right thing. Taking a trip to the spirit world in his mind might not be such a good idea. On the other hand, maybe there would be some good advice waiting for him on the other side.

At any rate, it sure beat counting sheep.

The word made him think of the Shepherds, and the Shepherds made him think of dark matter, and thinking of dark matter made anger swell, hot and full, inside his gut. That made his decision for him. He needed some help, and it was time to ask for it.

In his eagerness he wanted simply to seize the *akoonah* and get right to the heart of the thing, as he had done on his first vision quest so many years ago. But the older Chakotay, despite this strange anger and resentment that burned inside him like a stoked fire, knew that the experience would be enriched by the care taken in assembling the implements.

He unfolded the small fur blanket, letting his hands caress the smooth feathers of the blackbird's wing and linger over the carvings etched in the river stone. Chakotay breathed deep and composed himself.

"*Akoochimoya*. We are far from the sacred places of our grandfathers. We are far from the bones of our people. But perhaps there is one powerful being who will embrace this man and give him the answers he seeks."

He placed his hand on the *akoonah* and concentrated on the stone. The familiar tingling sensation crept through his hand. It was comforting, and Chakotay responded. He could feel the muscles in his back and neck unknotting as if being manually untied by an unseen presence. He took a deep breath and released it slowly, letting it trickle through his nostrils. Peace enveloped him. He opened his eyes.

He was surprised at the sight that greeted him. Always before, his spirit guides had met him in the lushness of a tropical rain forest or the cool comfort of a wooded glen. This, too, was a wild place, but as unlike the jungle or forest as could be imagined.

Chakotay stood in a desert.

The air was hot and he found it hard to breathe. Even as he blinked against the searing brightness of a cruel sun, a wind rose and bore the sand with it. It scoured his body and he bent over, trying to shield his faces from the merciless grains. A high-pitched howl rose. It was the sound of the wind itself. Or was it?

Chakotay tried to breathe and got a mouthful of grit for his efforts. His body, sweating in a desperate attempt to cool itself, was caked with the stuff. He coughed, and for a frantic moment he wondered what would happen to his real body, the one sitting cross-legged in the cool, quiet safety of his quarters aboard *Voyager,* if his mind thought he died here in the spirit realm. He'd never thought to ask Kolopak that particular nasty question, and fear swelled inside him.

"Oh, just cut that out," came an impatient voice.

Abruptly the howling wind stopped. The grains of sand fell back to earth, obeying the law of gravity even here in Chakotay's mind. He gasped in air and wiped at his grit-encrusted eyes.

In front of him, sitting on its haunches, its mouth open as if it were laughing at him, sat a coyote.

This was not good. This was not good at all. Coyote was the Trickster. Chakotay yearned for his friend, the wise if occasionally infuriating snake, or some of the other animals who had come to him when he needed their aid. He'd never before encountered Coyote.

"Aw," said Coyote mockingly. It tilted its head to the side. "Not happy to see me?"

Its voice, Chakotay realized with a further sensation of dread, was that of Q.

"So right now you're wondering, is Q Coyote, or is Coyote Q, and just what the hell am I doing conjuring up either one of them at a time like this? Am I right?" Coyote flipped over and wriggled into the sand, all four paws in the air. "Oooh, that feels good. Care to try it?"

"No. Thank you," he added as an afterthought. It wouldn't do to offend Coyote. "But you are correct about one thing. I'm not certain why you're here. I'm in trouble. We all are. We need some help."

"I'm a coyote, not a doctor," snarled the creature. It sat up and busily shook out the sand from its fur. "Besides, I'm not even real. And you expect me to find a cure?"

The anger, the heavy, hot anger, was rising. Chakotay tried to fight it. "I wasn't asking for a cure, just for some help. I have my own burden to bear, and I'd like some assistance in handling it."

"Goodness, what a great big crybaby you are," said Coyote. "Perhaps you'd be better off not suffering anymore."

And it launched itself at him.

All Chakotay had time to register was yellow eyes, yellow teeth, and fetid breath. Instinctively he thrust his arms up, and cried out in pain as Coyote's teeth ravaged them. He struggled, but the beast seemed to grow in front of his eyes. Teeth snapped shut inches from his face, and the anger swelled and burst inside him. With a roar, Chakotay ceased defending himself and began to attack. His powerful hands reached out, closed on Coyote's thickly ruffed throat, and began to squeeze. The animal's tongue lolled, and its eyes rolled back into its skull. It went limp.

Still Chakotay pressed on, choking the creature until it was limp as a fur piece. Only then did he realize what he had done, the abomination, the sacrilege he had committed. He splayed his fingers and pulled them back from the creature's body as if Coyote were red-hot, threw his head back, and howled in anguish.

When he opened his eyes, Chakotay found himself back in his quarters, his face wet with tears.

The dark matter. Had it conjured up Coyote, or had that been a true part of his quest? Was he supposed to attack it, or let it envelop him in a symbolic death and, one hoped, rebirth? He was certain, however, that one was not supposed to kill one's spirit guide.

Unless it wasn't one's guide at all.

There were too many questions, all with unsettling answers. Too rattled to close the ceremony properly, Chakotay thrust the objects back into the medicine bundle and shoved the whole thing back in the drawer. He was wet with sweat and was trembling, and when sleep finally came to him, he dreamed of sand dunes and the yellow eyes of the Trickster.

Telek had been up for . . . he didn't know how long. Captain Janeway had kept him company for several hours as they began the painstaking and perhaps eventually futile attempt to reconfigure the sensors to pick up any trace of Shepherd activity. Seven of Nine had stayed even longer. Telek found that he felt remarkably comfortable around the former Borg. During the quiet hours while the rest of the crew of *Voyager* slumbered, he coaxed the attractive female into telling him about the Borg.

That was a revelation. Telek had never thought of himself as a man with an overactive imagination, but he didn't think even the famed Storyspinners of Tikal Province on Romulus could have come up with a more frightening tale. Creatures who were half organic, half machine, who existed solely to convert others to their likeness, to "assimilate" without thought, without question—the idea was terrifying.

He imagined some might liken the Romulan instinct for conquest to the Borg's abominable assimilation, but there were profound differences. Romulans were individuals, and respected individuality.

They wanted to bring other worlds into the fold, it was true, to exchange knowledge or tools for the powerful and often desirable cloak of Romulan protection. But surely that could not be held equal to the Borg's abominable practice of assimilation!

At last, even the indomitable Seven of Nine grew weary and retired to her regeneration chamber. Telek was left alone to pursue his task. He noticed that the security guard who had been a constant presence since he first arrived on the ship had been quietly reassigned. The gesture moved him. These people trusted him.

Of course, he mused, the minute he attempted to meddle with the computers or any of the ship's systems without express permission, he'd be arrested and thrown in the brig, so perhaps it wasn't as complete a gesture of trust as he'd like.

He chuckled, rubbed his tired eyes, and resumed his work.

His life, over the last several months, had revolved around the Shepherds the way Romulus revolved around its central star. If anyone knew the Shepherds, it was Telek R'Mor. He knew them even more intimately than did Chairman Kaleh, for he was the one with whom Lhiau and, less often, another Shepherd worked on a daily basis. He had learned to recognize their smell, sense their presence, decipher their muttered whisperings. While he was working on the wormholes, trying to find something he desperately did not want to find, Telek observed and noted and analyzed these beings responsible for both his success in his field and for the obliteration of the true timeline, and he had committed every scrap of information to memory.

It was by such focused and subtle eavesdropping that Telek had learned that the Shepherds with whom he was working so closely were not representative of all members of their race. Lhiau was so egotistical that it was with difficulty that he managed to conceal his contempt for his "softer" fellows. It was these other, more benevolent Shepherds whom Telek R'Mor hoped to contact.

Of course, it was possible, perhaps even probable, that he would pick up traces of the darker Shepherds and not their more moral colleagues. After all, it was Lhiau and his kind who had initiated contact with the Romulans. The other Shepherds might be so distant, perhaps not even existing in this time and space, that it would be impossible to contact them. But that was a risk he felt was—

Suddenly Telek felt queasy. The room began to spin and his stomach roiled. His vision darkened. He had never felt so ill in his life. He rose, and promptly toppled to the floor as the room seemed to turn upside down. He closed his eyes; that was somewhat better.

Taking slow, even breaths, it was with trembling fingers that he pressed the combadge Captain Janeway had pinned on his chest.

"Telek R'Mor to sickbay," he managed. "Medical emergency. Please send security guards to escort me."

In the end, they hadn't merely escorted R'Mor to sickbay. The two men in mustard and black had been forced to literally carry the Romulan, as his dizziness was so profound he hadn't even been able to stand on his own.

The Doctor scanned him with the medical tricorder. "I think you know what I am going to say."

Lying on the bed, his eyes tightly closed, Telek replied, "The dark matter has entered my cerebellum and is interfering with my balance."

"Precisely." The Doctor pressed a hypospray to the Romulan's neck. "This should neutralize the damage for a few hours. However, you know as well as I do that—"

"The dark matter is spreading and multiplying, and as yet we have determined no way to halt it." The overarching metal receded into the bed and Telek sat up. "Thank you for stabilizing the world for me, Doctor. It was becoming quite . . . distracting."

The Doctor's holographic lips thinned. "I'm seeing more and more of this every hour. Lieutenant Carey's bones are disintegrating. Ensign Wildman has a heart arrhythmia. Seven's implants are giving her trouble. And of course there's Neelix. The prognosis is not good, Dr. R'Mor."

The Romulan regarded him evenly. "And it will only become worse, unless we can find the entities who know how to control the dark matter. Thank you again, Doctor. Your treatment may have bought us the chance we need. Everything depends on my being able to find the Shepherds."

The Doctor hesitated, then said softly, "I have found critical errors in my program. For the most part I have been able to bypass them. Lieutenant Torres has designed a subroutine that enables her to rewrite certain aspects of my program once an error is detected. But . . . ."

He did not have to say anything more. The Doctor was a sort of firebreak for this imperiled crew. He might not be able to cure the ills caused by the alien matter inside their bodies, but he could mitigate the damage it caused. If he ceased to function, they were all doomed.

Telek rose, nodded, and returned to his post in Astrometrics. Fear provided the needed adrenaline now, fear at his own close call.

He fed information, clue by clue, to the no doubt exhausted Lieutenant Torres. Finally, after another two hours had passed, her weary voice floated to him from the combadge.

"Torres to R'Mor."

"R'Mor here."

"Well, it's as close as I can get it." A hint of defensiveness. "I don't know if it's going to do you any good."

"It could do us a universe of good, Lieutenant. I thank you for your efforts. I will let you know when I have found any trace of Shepherd activity."

Silence. Telek knew that most of the *Voyager* crew thought his effort to find the Shepherds was a futile one. But it was the only thread they had to cling to. Otherwise, they would have to surrender to the ravages of the dark matter, and that was not an option.

"Sleep now, Lieutenant," he said, his voice gentle. "I will take over from here."

"Okay. Good night."

The sensors of this mighty ship, twenty years ahead of any technology he had ever known other than that of the mysterious Shepherds, were now his to command. Telek entered the data with hands that trembled. Calling upon his memory, he tapped in frequencies, resonances, any and all anomalies that he had associated with the Shepherds in any way. Finally he finished, and waited for the sensors to complete their scan.

Telek stretched. His joints popped. He was exhausted, but the knowledge inside his head was the one thing that might save them all. It would no doubt take a long time for the sensors to locate any of the discrepancies in space-time he had requested. He would linger here a few more moments, to catch any immediate errors he might have entered, then return to his quarters.

To sleep, again alone, as he had for far too long now. As he would for the rest of his life. The pain surged in his abdomen, welling forth with surprising rawness. If he could only save this ship, this crew, perhaps his family would not have died in vain.

He forced himself to redirect his thoughts. Dark matter. One of the last, great mysteries of the cosmos. Perhaps, if—no, when—they contacted the Shepherds, that mystery would finally be revealed to him. They understood dark matter. They knew what it was. Of course, theories abounded, and everyone knew them. Telek's favorite theory was the shadow matter theory. This held that there was another universe that was related to our own only through gravity. There were shadow people, shadow planets, just like those in the more familiar universe.

It was not a particularly imaginative theory, but Telek liked it. It had already been proved that other, alternate universes existed. He thought about the so-called mirror universe, where everything was perverted, where good was evil, and everything was dark. No doubt Jekri Kaleh would thrive in such an environment.

The console began to flash. Telek sat upright so quickly he almost fell out of his chair.

"On screen," he told the computer.

At once, the dark screen was filled with light and color. Lines chased themselves across the blackness, forming shapes.

"Frequency identified as emanating from the sixth planet of the star system located in Sector 6837," intoned the computer.

For a long moment, Telek merely stared. He could not believe it. Surely there must have been a miscalculation. The universe was a rather large place. For him to have found traces of Shepherd activity this quickly was impossible.

Unless Shepherd presence was far, far more pervasive than anyone had thought.

Telek tapped his combadge. "Telek R'Mor to Captain Janeway."

"Janeway here." The response was immediate. He suspected she hadn't been sleeping.

"Captain." He licked his lips. "Captain. I have . . . I have found the Shepherds."

"I must confess," said Janeway a scant fifteen minutes later, "that I didn't think you'd actually find anything."

"Neither did I," Telek confessed. "At least, not so quickly."

The entire senior staff had gathered in Astrometrics. To one degree or another, thought their captain, they all looked exhausted. Drained. As if the life energy were being sucked out of them by a parasite—which, she thought, wasn't an inappropriate analogy.

The nightmare was still with her. She couldn't seem to shake the damn thing. Ruthlessly she forced it from her mind and tried to focus.

"So you are suggesting that we change course and travel to this planet."

Telek frowned. "I believe that was the entire purpose of this exercise, Captain—to locate the Shepherds and seek them out, to ask for their aid."

"I had hoped—" Janeway caught herself. She didn't want to sound plaintive or appear distrustful of Telek. "No one expected to be able to locate the Shepherds so easily. I'd thought we might use the time to keep experimenting, run a few more tests. This ship is in trouble, just as its crew is. That planet you've found isn't exactly around the corner. Ever since we realized what's been going on we've been traveling at impulse power. Who knows what going to warp will do to *Voyager?* It could damage the antimatter containment field, we could lose our artificial gravity or the structural integrity field—"

"All of which will mean nothing if we are captured by the Romulans or go mad," said Chakotay, quietly. He did not often contradict her in public, and Janeway glared at him.

He met her gaze evenly. There were dark circles under his eyes. "Telek has told us that his encryption probably won't hold up under Tal Shiar scrutiny. And once they've got his formulas, they can begin hunting us again. We're sitting ducks if we stay in the same area of space."

The image of a fatally damaged *Voyager* filled Janeway's mind. After a fashion, she loved every member of this crew. No one else knew just how badly it hurt her when she lost one of them, how deeply she grieved in private, how she questioned her decisions in the solitude of her quarters.

And there were a few on this ship she loved probably more than she ought to.

The thought of *Voyager* shaking itself to bits, or exploding, taking not only her but these unique, special people with it . . . .

Her lips moved, but she couldn't speak. A crippling sense of helpless indecision washed over her. Chakotay saw the fear blossom in her eyes, and his tired-looking face softened with compassion.

"Captain," he said, and motioned her aside. In a hushed voice that the others could not hear he asked, with infinite gentleness, "Is the dark matter affecting your judgment, Captain? There is no shame in admitting an illness if your crew will be the better for it."

She gazed into his dark eyes, and found words. "Yes," she said, in a voice as soft as his. "But I know it for what it is. I can still fight this battle, Chakotay. I still know what I need to do, and I'll do it."

Janeway turned to go, but Chakotay caught her arm. "If the battle becomes too much—"

"There's no one I'd rather give my sword to," she replied, with what she hoped was a reassuring smile. She took a deep breath, straightened, and strode back to the rest of the group. They looked at her expectantly.

"I'll destroy *Voyager* before I see it fall into the hands of the Romulans," Janeway declared. "Too much is at stake to permit that. The Doctor tells me that every moment we allow the dark matter to work its malice on our bodies and our vessel, we're that much closer to death—or worse. We're dealing with a complete unknown. The ship could fall apart when we go into warp, or it could be just fine. Or it could fall apart at any moment for no reason at all. The Shepherds could cure us with a wave of their hands, or they could kill us where we stand. We simply don't know. But that's the name of the game, isn't it?"

She looked around, fixing every face in her mind. "One thing is certain. Delay is fatal. Only action will save us. Tom, when we return to the bridge, I want you to enter a course that will take us directly to the sixth planet of Sector 6837. At warp five. Understood?"

Paris glanced uneasily at Telek, then nodded. "Yes, ma'am."

Janeway felt something tight inside her relax just a little. The decision had been made. A slow smile spread across her face.

"Then let's go find those Shepherds."

CHAPTER

7

"Two of Four to Flotter."

"Flotter here."

"Report."

"The crew is experiencing quite a morale lift, now that we are going after the Shepherds. I don't know who they are, though."

Two of Four frowned at her adjunct. "That information is distributed on a need-to-know basis. Obviously, you do not need to know."

Naomi made the doll's head nod in reluctant agreement, even as she struggled with her own feelings of being left out. Why hadn't anyone told her who the Shepherds were? Why were they so important? Still, as she told Flotter, she supposed it didn't really matter. Everyone seemed much more hopeful now that the news—whatever it was—was spreading among the crew.

Morale. That was Uncle Neelix's job. Maybe when they found the Shepherds, they'd be able to cure him.

Tears threatened again, but Naomi blinked them back. She stood straight and pretended to examine the "weapons" she'd cobbled together from broken pieces of various downed shuttlecraft. Captain Janeway had permitted her to take a few bits and pieces for just such a purpose the last time one of the shuttlecraft was damaged. Now that she thought about it, that did seem to happen a lot on *Voyager.*

Imitating what she'd been able to glean from shrewd observation and the occasional sneak peak at the computer, Two of Four announced, "The weapon is completely operational. Flotter, prepare to examine the room for any sign of—"

Darn it, she'd lost the word again. That was happening to her a lot—forgetting things. Naomi hadn't said anything to anyone; she was afraid to. Now and then she'd summon her courage, start to talk to her mother about it, and then close her mouth at her mother's angry retorts. Mama didn't use to snap at her like that.

Once, Naomi had actually gone down to sickbay on her own, but she had forgotten where she was going before she got there. When she remembered, she had, again, decided not to pursue it.

But it was awfully frustrating when—

"Intruders." That was the word. She held the "weapon" in her right hand, its "barrel" pointed down toward the floor in proper safety position, and moved as silently and gracefully as she could through the cargo bay. All was, of course, as she had left it, up to and including her makeshift "regeneration chamber." Nobody else came down here very often.

Then she frowned, warring with her erratic memory. That bin—didn't it used to be over there? And the little space that was cleared—it was big enough for someone to sit down.

Or was her memory just playing tricks? Had she, yesterday, moved the bins herself?

Naomi didn't think so.

Slowly, she put down the toy weapon and moved toward the bins. She placed her shoulder against one and pushed. She couldn't budge it more than a couple of inches, even when she squeezed her eyes shut and grunted with effort. Nope. She certainly hadn't moved it and forgotten she'd done so.

"Somebody's been sneaking into our room!" she told Flotter indignantly. Someone was spying on her, maybe right this minute. Naomi glanced up and looked around, saw nothing unto—unto—wrong.

Her small mouth thinned. She was angry at the thought of some nosy grown-up creeping into her private area and snooping on her. She'd show them. She'd set a trap for the intruder.

Steeling herself for the pain, she plucked several long hairs from her scalp. "Ouch," she muttered as she examined the hairs and rubbed her stinging head. Yes, they would do. Working carefully, Naomi strung the long hairs directly across the path that led to the cleared area. There was no wind or anything else here that might break them. Only someone crossing this thin line would snap the hairs.

Satisfied, she stood up. She'd check back shortly to see if her unknown snoop had returned.

Tom rubbed his gritty eyes and fought back a yawn. If the captain caught him nodding, he'd be relieved of duty. Never mind that he was pulling a second shift. They were finally *doing* something about this damned dark matter and Paris wanted to be on the bridge when they contacted these Shepherds.

Intellectually, Paris understood that his short temper and suspicion of Telek R'Mor were due to the malignant matter inside his body. Intellectually. He'd seen the stuff on the Doc's screens in sickbay, and in calmer moments could even distinguish between his ordinary thoughts and his panicky, paranoid flights of fancy. Hell, he'd seen what the mutated crap had done to Neelix . . . Neelix! The gentlest, sweetest guy on the whole ship.

But that didn't mean the feelings were any less real to him.

Even now, his hand crept down to his belly and scratched. He could have sworn he could *feel* the stuff inside him, moving around in his bloodstream, in the liquids between the cells—

Cut it out, Tom. That's the dark matter talking.

He closed his eyes briefly, took a deep breath, and opened them again.

He was looking forward to this routine exercise.

Combat practice always got the blood flowing. Paris was not the best scholar at the Academy, but he always scored high points in combat exercises. The love of a pilot for the vessel. Too bad he'd missed out on the Cardassian conflict, but hey, he could pretend. Add a little life to the routine run.

Yes, here he was, Pilot Tom Paris, about to tackle the dangerous Cardassian warship. A smile touched his lips. Sure, it was make-believe, but it was fun.

"Let's do it," he said.

(What was that, Ensign?) The female voice seemed to come from very far away and it was so easy to ignore.

He took the ship into a dive . . .

(Ensign! What the—)

. . . and imagined that the Cardassian ship opened fire. *Keep the nose down, that's it, wait, wait for the best shot—*

Fire! Pull up, pull up—

And then he realized that he'd taken the formation too low, held the dive too long—

(Override! Override!)

From upside down in a spiraling escape run, Paris watched three friends die, one after the other. He was the only one who had had enough time to escape death. They didn't have a chance.

My fault. My fault. I was the team leader. What the hell was I doing? Oh God, oh God—

Hands seized his shoulders and dragged him away from the conn. Someone slipped into his chair and brought the vessel—brought *Voyager*—back on an even keel.

Chakotay held one arm, Tuvok the other. Tom blinked sweat out of his eyes. His heart was going a kilometer a minute.

Captain Kathryn Janeway, who had so abruptly taken his seat, whirled to glare at him.

"What the hell were you doing, Ensign?" Her blue eyes flashed and her lips were thin with outrage.

Tom could only stare, not at his captain, but at the screen over her shoulder. No asteroid, no floating bits of debris that had once been the three people dearest to him in the universe. Memory came back, memory of who and where he was now. He'd just whipped *Voyager* around like a child's plaything while it was at full warp speed. He could have killed everyone.

Just like he killed his friends.

Tears made his vision blur. Chakotay and Tuvok had hauled him to his feet, and Janeway strode toward him until her face was mere centimeters from his.

"What were you doing, Tom?" she asked coldly.

"I . . . I was doing combat practice back at the Academy," Tom managed. "The one where . . . the accident—"

His throat closed up and refused to utter any more words. He stared helplessly at Janeway.

Janeway's face softened. "Oh," was all she said. Then, "I wish I had the luxury of confining you to quarters. I'll be frank with you. I'm not at all comfortable with the idea that my conn officer is having flashbacks."

"Captain?" It was Tuvok. Janeway raised a hand, forestalling the Vulcan's protests.

"We're all affected by the dark matter right now," she said. "The Doctor can compensate. Who's to say that the second-shift conn officer might not have worse symptoms than Mr. Paris? No, Ensign, I want you to report to sickbay and give the Doctor a full report of everything that happened up here. Unless he pronounces you utterly unfit for duty, I want you back here on the bridge. Understood?"

Tom did understand. Not just her orders, but the gift she was giving him. He wasn't sure just why she was being so, well, compassionate about this, but he wasn't about to look a gift horse in the mouth.

"Understood, Captain."

Not even an hour had passed, but Naomi was bored and the mysterious intruder was all she could think about. Her mom was busy working, Neelix was—and the Doctor had told her he was far too busy to continue with her lessons.

She stepped inside the cargo bay and at once she noticed something by the moved bins. Something glittered in the dim light. Absently she plopped Flotter down on a bin near the entrance. He fell over slowly. Her attention completely caught, Naomi didn't think to check if her little hair trap had been sprung. What were these things? She didn't recognize them at all. She had just reached to touch one of the shiny crystal spheres when the door to the cargo bay hissed open.

Even though Naomi knew she hadn't done anything wrong, she gasped and whirled, her heart racing. Quickly she ducked behind two other large bins a couple of feet away, not knowing why she did so. Cautiously, she peered around the bin, trying to see who had intruded upon her little sanctuary.

There was no one else in the room.

The door shut. Naomi frowned, but then her puzzlement turned to an icy fear when she heard footsteps moving in her direction. They stopped, and to her utter horror she watched as Flotter was lifted into the air about half a meter. He hung there, grinning, for several seconds. Naomi gaped, too enthralled to look away.

A male voice chuckled, then Flotter was set down. The footsteps resumed.

There was still no one else in the room.

Naomi crouched back, fighting back a whimper of fear. What was going on? Was she going crazy, like Neelix?

The footsteps came closer. They passed right by Naomi's hiding place and continued on for a few more steps until they reached the cleared area that Naomi had been examining only a few moments earlier. As before with Flotter, the curious trinkets she had touched suddenly rose into the air.

Then they vanished.

Scuffling noises ensued, a rough voice spoke in a language Naomi had never heard. There were sounds that seemed familiar, though she couldn't place them—beeps, clicks, hisses. Then the footsteps began again, this time heading back toward the door. From her hiding place, Naomi watched as the door hissed open, then closed again.

She hardly dared breathe.

Voyager had a ghost.

"Naomi Wildman." Seven glanced up from the console as the little girl rushed inside.

"Seven!" gasped Naomi. "I know you won't believe it, but it's true, and I have to tell somebody and—"

"Naomi Wildman. Calm yourself," said Seven flatly. "Speak slowly and in complete sentences."

Naomi gulped. Seven noticed that the girl's face was flushed, and sweat had begun to gather at her hairline. With an effort, the child composed herself.

"I was playing in the cargo bay—not yours, the other one—because I'm not allowed on the holodeck anymore. I'd set up—" Naomi stopped in midsentence, then continued. "I'd set up kind of a play fort. You know."

"No," said Seven honestly, "I do not. Elaborate."

Naomi squirmed. This part of the conversation obviously made her uncomfortable. Seven did not understand why, and her frown deepened with every second Naomi hesitated. The girl saw the expression on her face and rushed to continue.

"I'd moved some boxes around, and made some toys and stuff. It's a special place just for me. I go there to play and be by myself."

"Ah," said Seven, comprehending. "A regeneration chamber."

Naomi giggled. Seven was puzzled. She was unaware that she had said anything humorous.

"Yes, that's it. A regeneration chamber. Anyway, I noticed that some really big boxes had been moved. So I set up a trap—strung some hairs between pieces of equipment. If whoever it was came back, I'd know."

Seven raised an eyebrow. "Inventive."

"So I checked back in an hour. I didn't get a chance to see if the hairs had been broken, but I did see some stuff there that I didn't recognize and then . . ." Naomi's voice faltered.

"Continue."

"The door opened, and I heard footsteps. But there was nobody there, Seven! I watched, I saw . . . and he lifted Flotter up and laughed at him. And then he left again. It's a ghost, Seven! We've got a ghost on board!"

Naomi's wild story no longer interested Seven. She returned her attention to the console. Although the leap into warp had not damaged the ship—at least as far as they could tell—constant monitoring was required to avert any possible disasters. She did not have time to listen to Naomi's tales.

"There are no such things as ghosts."

"Commander Chakotay thinks there are."

"Then perhaps you should continue this conversation with Commander Chakotay. I am busy, Naomi. Return to your regeneration chamber."

Out of the corner of her eye, Seven noticed the girl's face crumple. What was the phrase the Doctor used the last time Seven had discussed Naomi? Her feelings had been "hurt," he had told her, as if emotions were a physical part of the body that could be damaged and then repaired. Seven sighed and turned to face her.

"You don't believe me," said Naomi in a low voice, staring at the floor. "You think I'm just making it up, just to get attention."

"No, I do not. You would not indulge in such self-aggrandizing behavior. You are more intelligent than that."

Naomi brightened. "But Seven, you know I wouldn't bother you if I hadn't really seen it."

"I believe you think you have seen it," said Seven, making a deliberate effort to soften her stance somewhat. "But you are aware of the dark matter that has permeated our bodies and is affecting our judgment. You have merely hallucinated this, or else you have created an imaginary friend."

Naomi planted her hands on her small hips and stared at Seven indignantly. "Why do I need to make up imaginary friends when I have the holodeck?"

Seven raised an eyebrow. "You do not have the holodeck at the moment."

Naomi stomped her foot. "Seven, I'm not!"

"What is it you require of me?" asked Seven, trying to pinpoint something concrete that the child wished her to do.

"I don't know. I just wanted to tell someone, I think." She peered up at Seven. "You really think it's the dark matter? That I hall—haloo—"

"Hallucinated."

"Hallucinated the ghost?"

"I do. What would a ghost be doing in a cargo bay? If I recall the myths correctly, ghosts manifest at the site where they were neutralized or in places they frequently visited before their deaths. No one on *Voyager* besides myself has any connection to the cargo bay whatsoever. No one lives there, and certainly no one has died there."

Her logic seemed to reach the child. Seven was pleased. She would have to tell the Doctor about this. He would undoubtedly compliment her on how well, how sensitively, she had handled the issue.

"Okay," said Naomi, having come to some sort of decision. "Thanks, Seven. Sorry to bother you."

Feeling gracious, Seven replied, "It is no bother," even though Naomi's interruption had, in truth, distracted Seven from her assigned tasks. She had found that these polite prevarications—Paris called them "little white lies"—were integral to smooth human interaction.

She did not watch as Naomi left, noting by the hissing of the door that the child had gone. Seven returned her attention to the screen. With a few deft touches, she commanded the computer to refresh the image.

There it was, the planet that Telek R'Mor had assured them bore the Shepherds. Seven frowned to herself. What a strange name to call one's race.

Her vision blurred. She blinked. It was occurring again, that jumpy, hazy image that filled her vision and then disappeared. It was the fourth time since she had assumed her post today that it had happened—once on the bridge, twice in various corridors, and now here in Astrometrics.

There had been incidents aboard *Voyager* where the crew had been affected by various illnesses or conditions, and Seven had been exempt, thanks to her implants. But it would seem that mutated dark matter did not discriminate. It occurred to Seven that if there were a way to infect the Borg Queen with this substance, the Borg threat would be eliminated forever.

The image came again: an area approximately two meters in height and one meter in length shimmered and danced across her field of vision.

A cursory glance at the screen told Seven there was no immediate threat to the ship that would require her attention. Nonetheless, it was with reluctance that she tapped her combadge.

"Seven of Nine to sickbay. My ocular implant requires adjustment."

"Again?" The Doctor's exasperation came clearly through the commlink.

"Again," stated Seven as she headed out the door.

Naomi hesitated at the door of the cargo bay. She thought Seven was one of the smartest people she'd ever met. If Seven thought the dark matter was affecting her judgment, then that's probably exactly what was happening. Naomi knew she ought to report to sickbay, but the last time she'd peeked in the Doctor seemed to have his hands full and spoke crossly to people. Besides, she'd left Flotter here, and if she wasn't going to come back any more—

and the cargo bay was fast losing its appeal—then she wanted to retrieve him.

Still she lingered just outside, peering in. She glanced around. Everything was as she had left it, including the moved bins. There was Flotter, perched atop a bin where—

—where the ghost had put him. Naomi swallowed, and all of Seven's cool, soothing words evaporated like mist.

"I imagined it," she said in a fierce whisper, hoping that uttering the words aloud would make them true. "The—"

She forgot what it was that was making her hall—hall—see things that weren't there. But Seven had said it, so it must be correct.

Slowly, Naomi walked forward. Flotter grinned up at her. Trembling, she reached out and touched the toy. It felt exactly as it always had—soft and slightly furry. This, at least, had not changed. Quickly she snatched up Flotter and squeezed him tightly.

Yes, she had just imagined it. And as for the bins, well, someone had clearly needed something and come in and gotten it. That happened all the time in a cargo bay aboard a starship. Of course it did.

Then Naomi remembered the hairs she'd strung between the bins. She could believe that someone might have come in earlier to move the bins to get a needed article, but they certainly hadn't been back. Nothing else was disturbed. If they'd come back, the bins would have been moved again. So it stood to reason that the hairs would still be in place.

Don't look, she told herself. *Just don't look.* If she didn't look, she wouldn't know, could just go on thinking it was her imagination.

But Naomi could no more refrain from checking than she could cease breathing. It was in her nature. She had spent all of her brief life asking questions, learning, looking, growing, and she had to know for certain if there was a ghost aboard *Voyager* or if she needed to turn right around and march herself to sickbay.

She held Flotter in front of her like a shield. She swallowed hard, took a deep breath, and with a steadiness to her movements that she didn't feel in the pit of her stomach, stepped forward toward the moved bins.

The hairs were gone.

Naomi gasped. She'd been right the first time. But oddly enough, she felt more excited than afraid. Once, after a bad nightmare experienced when her mom had come so close to death, Naomi had spoken with Commander Chakotay about ghosts and spirits. She'd been a little afraid of him once, he being so big and all, but his voice was soft and his movements gentle. He'd told her that ghosts weren't evil, that they were just people who'd gotten stuck in this life when they were supposed to pass on to another place. Ghosts needed help to pass on. He'd then launched into a description of an elaborate releasing ritual, which had utterly enthralled Naomi at the time but which now she could not remember. One thing she did recall, though. Ghosts sometimes needed someone to speak to them, so they could tell their sad stories.

"Mr. Ghost," she said softly, looking around for— what? "M-my name is Naomi Wildman. I'm very sorry you're stuck here. Is there anything I can do to help you get unstuck?"

Silence. But not an empty silence. Now that Naomi knew he—for it was a male; she'd heard him laugh at Flotter—was real, she could sense him. Her skin and scalp prickled, though the temperature didn't drop as she had half expected from Commander Chakotay's tales.

"Hello? I know you're here. I—"

From out of nowhere, a hand clamped down on her mouth. Another one seized her arm and dragged her forward. She didn't even have time to scream.

CHAPTER

8

"I WISH YOU'D STOP WASTING MY TIME," GROWLED THE Doctor.

Seven was surprised. She knew that most of the crew complained about the Doctor's lack of something dubbed "a bedside manner" in the vernacular, but any brusqueness the Doctor displayed usually didn't bother her. Today, however, he was unusually rough in his handling of her, and even Seven by now knew true rudeness when she heard it.

"Doctor, you have instructed me to report any and all malfunctions with—"

"Seven, you are not malfunctioning!" exploded the Doctor. "You are not damaged or malfunctioning or any other mechanical term you'd care to use. There is nothing wrong with your implants. Nothing. N-o-t-h-"

"I can spell," Seven replied, a hint of annoyance

creeping into her own throat. Her chest hurt a little. She realized that the Doctor's attitude, which was completely inexplicable, was "hurting her feelings." Illogical though it was, emotional distress did cause physical pain.

"Why do you say there is nothing wrong?" she asked, slipping off the table to confront him. "I have told you, from time to time I see a distortion of objects. It does not occur in the eye without the implant, therefore it must be—"

"All in your head," interrupted the Doctor, flicking a finger against the metal of her ocular implant. "The dark matter is probably responsible. It seems that everything around here can be rationalized away by the dark matter."

"I am hallucinating?" The thought did not sit well with her.

"Indeed. Now go away and let me attend to the patients who actually need treatment."

Again she experienced the odd pang in her chest. Seven deliberately forced her emotions down. "How is Naomi Wildman?" she inquired.

He was busy arranging his surgical tools, though Seven noted that they were in perfect alignment. They lay on the tray, separated by approximately 0.35 centimeters of space. The Doctor frowned, picked up his autosuture, and moved it a tiny bit closer to the cortical stimulator. Seven recognized this as obsessive behavior, but kept her own counsel.

"Naomi?" He frowned. "I haven't seen her for quite some time. Why do you ask?"

"She too was having hallucinations. She was playing in her regenerator in the cargo bay and imagined she saw and heard an intruder."

He looked concerned at that. "In a child, the degeneration caused by the dark matter could progress much more rapidly. I'd better see her." He tapped his combadge. "Sickbay to Naomi Wildman."

Silence. Frowning, the Doctor tried again. "She's not responding. She could be sick or injured. Seven, you know all the nooks and crannies where she likes to play. Find her and escort her to sickbay."

Seven was less worried than the Doctor, but she agreed. It would do Naomi some good to undergo a thorough examination. It would take her mind off her imaginary friend.

"Seven tells me you're just an imaginary friend," said Naomi, sitting cross-legged beside Mr. Ghost. "Or else I was hallucinating. But *I* knew you were real."

"Yes," replied her new friend. "I am indeed real. But you must not tell anyone else about me. Let them think you're just a simple child, imagining a playmate. We can know better. It can be our special secret."

Naomi grinned and hugged Flotter. "Okay! It'll be nice to have someone to play with."

"Now, Naomi," chided Mr. Ghost, "you understand that being a ghost is not a trifling matter. I have many . . . ." He paused, and his ridged brow furrowed. "Many rites of atonement to perform in order to . . . to pass on."

At once, Naomi sobered. "Oh. I suppose you do. Is there anything I can get you?"

"Nothing right now—only your silence, Naomi. If you tell anyone about me, then I will be set back in my attempts to pass on. You wouldn't want to do that to me?"

"Oh no!" She shook her head so vigorously that her hair flew. "I would never—"

The door hissed open. Naomi gasped. Mr. Ghost got silently to his feet, his hand at the weapon on his belt. He signaled her to be quiet, and she nodded her comprehension.

Kneeling, he brought his lips to her ear and whispered, "The magic cocoon that hides me and my equipment will also hide you, if you are silent."

"Naomi Wildman?" It was Seven of Nine. Naomi rolled her eyes. A little while ago, she'd have been thrilled that Seven wanted to come and meet her ghost. Now, with Mr. Ghost's passage to the other world in jeopardy, Naomi wished with all her heart that Seven would just go away.

The former Borg strode inside and looked around. "Are you hiding in here, Naomi? If so, please cease doing so immediately. The Doctor has requested that you report to sickbay for a complete physical examination."

Naomi scowled. She hated being poked and prodded. She was now very glad that she was safe within Mr. Ghost's cocoon and Seven couldn't find her.

Her combadge chirped. "Sickbay to Naomi Wildman."

Naomi gasped and stared down at the betraying piece of equipment pinned to her chest. She'd heard the Doctor calling for her earlier and had simply ignored it. Now, though, it was going to get her in trouble.

Seven, too, had heard the Doctor's voice, and now her blond head whipped around and she began to move purposefully toward the cocoon. At a loss as to what to do, Naomi looked toward her new friend.

Calmly he plucked the offending combadge off Naomi's chest, placed it down, and sent it sliding along the floor so gently that it barely made any noise. It came to a stop a scant meter away from the edge of the cocoon. Naomi was flooded with admiration for Mr. Ghost's cleverness and gazed at him with a grin.

Again, the Doctor's voice issued forth. "Naomi, where are you?"

Seven followed the sound and squatted down to pick up the combadge. She examined it for a moment, then sighed in exasperation. It was the most human sound Naomi had ever heard her utter.

Tapping her own combadge, Seven said, "Seven of Nine to sickbay. I am in the cargo bay, Doctor, and I have located Naomi's combadge. She is not here."

"It's that mutated matter again," complained the Doctor. "The child probably took it off for some silly reason and forgot to put it back on again. I'll send security after her."

Seven rose, her metal-clad fingers running over the smooth surface of the badge. "Is that really necessary?"

"She's running loose without her combadge on a starship that could break down at any moment. Yes, I think it's necessary."

Seven raised an eyebrow but did not reply. "As you wish. I am returning to Astrometrics. Seven out."

Still holding Naomi's badge, Seven left the cargo bay. The door hissed shut behind her.

Naomi exhaled loudly. "You were so smart! That was close!"

"Yes," said her new friend, his dark eyes narrowing as he gazed after Seven. "It was. Perhaps you had best report to sickbay, Naomi. It would not do for them to have security out searching for you."

"But I don't want to leave you!" The childish wail was out before Naomi could stop it. She knew she sounded like a big baby, but she couldn't help herself. Perhaps the Doctor was right. Perhaps the—whatever it was inside her—was making her act imma—immature.

He turned to regard her, his ridged, raised brow cloaking his dark eyes in shadow, making them look even darker. For the first time since he had grabbed her, Naomi felt a thrill of fear. Maybe ghosts weren't so harmless after all.

"I told you not to arouse suspicion. I have work to do. Do you want me to suffer eternal torment, unable to pass on?"

"N-no."

"Then do as I tell you, child." He took a deep, shuddering breath, and for an instant pressed his hand to his side, as if something hurt deep inside him.

"Are you okay?"

"No. As you see, the torment is already beginning." His lips were thinned against the pain and his voice was harsh. "Go, Naomi. We will play again soon."

Reluctantly, Naomi obeyed. She would pretend she had simply wandered down to sickbay to visit the Doctor. It wouldn't do for them to know that she had heard them and deliberately kept hidden.

"Okay. But don't worry. I'll come back."

Mr. Ghost did not reply. He did not look well, that was for sure. Biting her lower lip, Naomi rose, walked through the invisible magic cocoon, and went to sickbay for her checkup.

It had happened to Seven of Nine again, while she was in the cargo bay. Her vision had shimmered in one certain spot, but she was not going to irritate the Doctor further by returning to sickbay. If this hallucination began to interfere with her work, then she would do so. In the meantime, she would turn her not inconsiderable powers of concentration to ignoring it.

B'Elanna felt sick. Very, very sick.

She envied Janeway's headache and Tom's paranoia. She'd trade her delicate stomach for either of those any day. She'd been to the Doctor, of course, and he had given her something that had made the queasiness subside. But he had also predicted it would return, and damn him, he'd been right.

As it was, B'Elanna had to walk slowly and deliberately and remember to breathe deeply. Any sudden movement made her stomach roil and threaten to void its contents, and Torres was determined with every ounce of human and Klingon pride that she was not, absolutely was not, going to throw up in front of Vorik, Carey, and the rest of engineering.

She felt all eyes on her as she walked carefully to the console. Vorik came up to her and asked solicitously, "Are you unwell, Lieutenant?"

"Yes," she replied honestly. "I'm sure you've got some problems of your own. Maybe you've got an earache or something." It was a deliberate insult and it came so naturally that B'Elanna winced.

Fortunately, it seemed that insults escaped the young Vulcan. "My ears are fine," he said, taking her words at face value. "However, I have noticed a slight loss in my manual dexterity."

"Oh, great. I'm going to be sick and you're going to punch the wrong button." She took a deep breath and pretended that her stomach was as fine as Vorik's ears. She needed to slide underneath the console to examine and probably replace yet another pair of damaged couplings and was uncertain as to what a supine position might do to her stomach.

She had just gotten to her knees when the ship rocked violently. Bile rose in her throat and she clapped a hand to her mouth, ferociously willing the contents of her stomach to stay right where they were. For the time being, they obeyed.

Seeing that his superior officer was in no condition to speak, Vorik tapped his combadge. "Vorik to bridge. What has occurred?"

"A miscalculation by Ensign Paris at the conn," came Chakotay's voice. "It's taken care of. There's nothing to worry about."

Sitting cross-legged on the engineering floor, still struggling to keep from vomiting, B'Elanna felt a chill. She knew Chakotay well enough to know that when he repeated a reassurance, it meant that there was indeed something to be worried about.

Tom. She hoped he was okay, but—

A sudden sound seized her attention. The console was beeping frantically. Adrenaline shot through Torres and she leaped to her feet, her stomach temporarily forgotten in the sudden flood of urgency.

Everyone knew what that sound meant and sprang into action. A warp core breach was imminent. Her mind became clear and focused. She realized that the emergency safeguards were failing to operate. Dimly, Torres heard Carey shouting something, heard Vorik contacting the bridge as she sprang to the console and manually activated the cylindrical forcefield that would isolate the engine from the rest of Engineering.

It didn't respond.

On to another console, to frantically tap in other commands. "Come on, come on," Torres muttered. The angry beeping and the wailing klaxon that indicated Red Alert numbed her ears. Sweat dampened her face, funneled away from her eyes by the ridges in her forehead. Her fingers danced, but their motion didn't feel quick enough to Torres. There. The emergency shutdown procedure would shut off all fuel feeds and activate magnetic quenching fields.

Except that didn't work, either. It was as if everything had been frozen.

Torres didn't waste another precious second fiddling with the controls. "Evacuate!" she screamed, waving her arms. "Everybody out, now, now, now, let's move it!"

Her heart thudding, she watched as her crew raced for the door. She'd acted in time; the last two people ran for it and Torres herself slammed a hand down on the controls that sealed off engineering and ran, literally, for her life.

The door descended. She wasn't going to make it! Grimly, Torres launched herself forward, landing hard on her stomach but sliding to safety just as the door slammed down centimeters from her toes. As Vorik and Carey helped her to her feet, she braced herself.

The sound was deafening, and the ship bucked. The emergency hatch at the bottom of the engineering hull blew off, and the entire warp reactor core was ejected into space. Just beyond the safety afforded by the closed door was the vacuum of space. If anyone had been a few seconds slower, she and they would be dead by now. Torres felt the adrenaline which had so efficiently fueled her ebb, leaving her weak and shaky.

"Carey," she said in a voice that trembled, "we've got to transfer the reserve warp engine core from its storage bay. You and I will—"

But apparently, she was not going to do anything with Carey, or Vorik, or anyone else in engineering.

She lost the battle she'd been fighting for the last few hours and was promptly violently sick.

"Dammit," growled Chakotay. "We're still light-years away from that Shepherd planet."

"Engineering, report," snapped Janeway.

"Almost all of the automatic systems failed," came Lieutenant Carey's voice. "We had to eject the core manually."

"Any casualties?"

"Torres got us all out safely."

Apprehension washed through the captain. Those words sounded ominous, and why wasn't Torres herself making the report?

"Is Lieutenant Torres safe?"

Janeway saw Paris's shoulders tense, but he said nothing. Good for him. She was glad she'd chosen to keep him on the bridge.

There was an awkward silence, then, "Captain, Lieutenant Torres is . . . indisposed. She's not injured, though. She's on her way to sickbay."

"Well, that's good news. What's the bad?"

"The warp core was ejected and should . . . Wait a minute. Captain, can you get it on screen?"

Kim had already done so, and Janeway and the rest of the bridge crew saw their ejected warp core turning slowly in space.

"I don't understand. The computer gave us all the warnings that the core was about to breach!" Carey sounded frustrated and utterly confused. "But it seems to be unharmed."

"I'd call that more good news than bad," said Janeway mildly, "though it's unnerving that we don't seem to be able to trust the computers. Paris, bring the ship about and let's go fetch our errant warp core." She glanced over at Chakotay. "We'll lose a few hours, but that's better than losing the entire core."

He didn't answer. His handsome face was set in a scowl, the tattoo on his brow furrowed by the frown. Janeway didn't pursue the conversation. The dark matter was affecting all of them, and she knew better than to take Chakotay's sullenness personally.

"I regret to say that I *can* offer some bad news," said Tuvok.

Janeway groaned and rubbed her throbbing temple. "What now?"

"The main weapons systems have also just gone off-line. And our shields are weakening as well."

Janeway closed her eyes, gathering her strength. Once, she'd hungered for knowledge of the mysteries of space. Dark matter had always intrigued her. But now, after having so personal an encounter with the stuff, she wished she'd never heard of it. It was crippling them, hamstringing them the way a pack of wolves hamstrung an elk to bring it down. Not a final, vicious attack, not yet; a little here, a little there, a headache, hallucinations, a quicker temper, the warp core ejected in error, the weapons systems down. Would they even make it to the Shepherd planet?

"Harry, prepare to record a message."

Kim thumbed the controls, then said, "Go ahead, Captain."

Janeway gazed at the slowly spinning warp core set against the light of stars in the blackness of space and spoke clearly and in full control.

"This is Captain Kathryn Janeway of the Federation *Starship Voyager.* This message is for the race of beings known to the Romulans as the Shepherds. Our ship and our bodies have been infected with mutated dark matter particles. We have detected your presence on the sixth planet in Sector 6837 and are attempting to rendezvous. We require your assistance. Our ship is damaged and we do not know if we can reach your planet before the damage becomes too great. Please contact us if you can help us."

She glanced over her shoulder at Kim. "Broadcast that message on all frequencies every three minutes, Ensign."

"With respect, Captain," Tuvok said, "if our weapons systems and shielding capabilities are not repaired quickly, we will be targets for any hostile forces in the area. We are announcing that we are defenseless."

Janeway smiled without humor. "If we don't get help soon, Tuvok, the point will be moot. Any system could go at any time, and if we can do anything to attract the Shepherds' attention, I'm all for it. Besides, we're a bit like an old-fashioned plague ship. Anyone who boards us or tries to acquire our technology runs a very substantial risk of being infected themselves." She glanced over her shoulder at her security officer. "Sometimes, Mr. Tuvok, you've just got to gamble."

Tuvok did not reply, but he did not look pleased, either.

"Janeway to Seven of Nine. I want your full attention on keeping the long-range sensors intact. If you notice anything unusual, report to me at once."

"Aye, Captain."

Janeway settled into her chair. There was nothing to do but wait.

In the corridor right outside engineering, safely away from the main flow of traffic, two ghosts spoke in whispers. Their task was nearing completion.

CHAPTER

9

"Ow!" Naomi yanked her arm back and glared at the Doctor. "That hurt!"

"Oh, it did not," replied the Doctor.

"It wasn't you who felt it!"

The Doctor sighed heavily. "Well, it's obvious your nervous system isn't impaired by the dark matter. Your brain, however, is another matter." He offered this assessment casually, as if he were commenting on a bruise she'd gotten while playing. "Pardon the pun," he added.

Naomi went cold. "My brain?" she echoed. "What's wrong with my brain?"

"The frontal area of your cortex is being targeted by the dark matter. The ribonucleic acid is failing to do its job of assisting memory storage.

Have you been suffering any short-term memory losses?"

Tears welled in her eyes. She was forgetting things? "No," she said, honestly. "Of course, I wouldn't remember if I forgot."

"Too true," sighed the Doctor. "I'm willing to bet that you are, though. Fortunately, that's not life-threatening."

Naomi was silent, fighting back tears. She was forgetting things. Who knew what wonderful memories were lost to her already? Through the haze of tears she looked around sickbay, and gasped when she saw a familiar figure lying still on the bed next to hers.

"Doctor! What's wrong with Uncle Neelix?"

The Doctor arched an eyebrow. "Definitely short-term memory loss," he said.

Captain's log, supplemental. Recovering the incorrectly ejected warp core is not a particularly dangerous or meticulous chore, but it is taking precious time. Tuvok and engineering keep reporting failures throughout the ship. At this point, we have no weapons and only ten percent of our normal shielding capacity. We are utterly vulnerable. We have heard nothing from the Shepherds, though Telek assures me that they are out there. They are our last hope.

The crew, too, is breaking down a piece at a time. It's all we can do to stay civil to one another. Having a goal—reaching the Shepherds' planet—has been

the glue that's held us together so far. If the Shep-
herds aren't there, or if they don't help us, then we
will be lost indeed.

Janeway thought about rerecording the log. Her
voice sounded so hollow, so hopeless. After debating
with herself for a moment, she decided to let it
stand. Nothing else would so eloquently convey the
stress and despair she was feeling, and in the future,
if—no, she corrected herself sternly, *when* they recovered from this and returned home, she wanted
those who had not undergone this ordeal to fully understand and appreciate it. Perhaps it would help the
Federation in the future, if anyone encountered mutated dark matter again.

"Seven of Nine to Captain Janeway."

"Janeway here. Go ahead, Seven, what is it?"

"I have detected an unauthorized transmission
emanating from the ship. The frequency is not standard Federation."

Adrenaline surged through her, rivaling even the
dreadful headache for Janeway's complete attention.
"Could it be a computer malfunction?"

"I suppose it is possible," said Seven, sounding
doubtful.

Janeway was doubtful, too. She rose and strode
onto the bridge as she spoke. "Where's the source?

The door hissed open and Telek R'Mor appeared
on the bridge. He looked agitated and opened
his mouth to speak, but Janeway waved him to silence.

"From Cargo Bay One," Seven replied. "Captain, Naomi Wildman has taken to playing there since you declared the holodeck off-limits. She spoke with me regarding an imaginary friend. Both the Doctor and I dismissed it as a hallucination, but perhaps—"

"Perhaps that friend wasn't so imaginary after all," finished Janeway. "Tuvok, Seven has detected—"

"I am aware of the transmission as well," said Tuvok.

"Captain!" Telek's voice was urgent. "The signals Seven has reported—I recognize the frequency. It's Romulan!"

Naomi was still in sickbay when Seven of Nine, Telek R'Mor, and Tuvok arrived there a scant ten minutes after Telek's stunning revelation.

"Naomi," said Seven without preamble, "does your imaginary friend look like Dr. R'Mor?"

Naomi gazed at her blankly. "I don't have an imaginary friend," she said, seeming puzzled.

"We spoke about it earlier," Seven said. Naomi showed no sign of recognition. "You said you thought that *Voyager* might be haunted. Surely you remember."

"She very well may be telling you the truth," interrupted the Doctor. "She's losing her short-term memory."

A wave of irritation washed through Seven. She had hoped that Naomi would be able to tell them something about their intruder.

"The child is of no help," said Telek.

"Neither were you," said Tuvok icily. "Why did you not inform us of the possibility we might be boarded?"

"Because I did not know of it," replied Telek angrily. "I have told you everything I was privy to. But I am not at all surprised that the Tal Shiar had other plans that they did not bother to share with a lowly scientist."

"One thing I do recall from my conversation with Naomi is that her alleged ghost was invisible." Seven looked at the Doctor. "You were correct, Doctor. My ocular implant was indeed functioning correctly. It was able to detect the presence of this intruder, although I did not realize what it was I was seeing. I am uncertain as to why it did so, however. It is not designed to identify and penetrate dark-matter shielding."

"I know you're in a hurry to find this fellow," said the Doctor, "but if you could spare a moment, I could adjust Seven's implant. She'd be able to see the not-so-imaginary friend more distinctly."

"Since Seven is the only person who can see the Romulan at all, I agree," Tuvok said. "I will instruct my security team to equip themselves with tricorders adjusted to scan on the infrared frequencies."

But Telek was shaking his head slowly. "If they have indeed managed to construct a personal cloak of dark matter, such adjustments will be of no help. We must search for high concentrations of dark matter and hope that the amounts already present aboard the vessel will not further confuse your equipment."

Telek was silent for a moment while the Doctor worked on Seven, then he said softly, "The fools! If only they had confided in me, I would have done more tests. I could have warned them."

Naomi Wildman was still watching them, her eyes flitting from one face to the other. Seven of Nine stood patiently while the Doctor readjusted her implant.

"Good hunting," he said when he had finished.

The ship's sensors and the tricorders proved to be of little value. They detected not one, but four large concentrations of the mutated dark matter, one of which was not even aboard *Voyager* but instead located immediately outside the vessel. Tuvok did not let his irritation show, but Seven of Nine knew him well enough by this point to be aware of it.

The team Tuvok had put together consisted of himself, Seven, Telek R'Mor—who, Seven noticed, was not equipped with a weapon—and three security guards, Ramirez, Johnson, and Kirby. They decided to investigate all four readings, although Tuvok felt certain that at least one, perhaps two, or even three were simply computer malfunctions. No one could trust the ship anymore.

They strode down the corridors to Cargo Bay One, where the transmission on the Romulan frequency had first been detected and, at least according to the tricorders, was still transmitting. Seven saw no ghosts, not now. She and the rest of the team obeyed Tuvok's silent commands to position themselves on either side of the door.

Slowly, Tuvok raised his hand and counted down on his fingers: *One. Two. Three.*

On "three" Tuvok leaped in front of the door, phaser at the ready. Seven was right behind him, her head turning this way and that, searching for the telltale distortion of space that would reveal the intruder and his dark-matter shield.

"There," she said, aiming her own phaser at an area that had been cleared of bins. With an odd sensation, she recalled that this particular spot had been Naomi Wildman's regeneration chamber.

"Surrender," stated Tuvok. There was no response. "There is no escape. Surrender and you will be treated fairly."

Again, silence.

Seven frowned. Her implants clearly showed a distortion of space. It did not move. "I do not think our intruder is present," she said. An idea was starting to take shape. She plucked her combadge from her chest, knelt, and with a quick movement of her wrist sent it skidding along the floor.

They all watched as the combadge suddenly disappeared.

"If I hadn't seen it with my own eyes . . . ." said Ramirez softly.

"He has erected a dark-matter shield to camouflage his activities and equipment," said Telek. "There must be something in there worth hiding. Tuvok, with your permission—"

"Denied," said Tuvok. "I will enter the shielded area and recover any equipment."

"You will be bombarded with particles of the dark matter. It will greatly accelerate any physical problems you may be having," warned Telek.

"I have experienced fewer problems than the rest of the crew," Tuvok replied. "Your knowledge of this substance makes you far too valuable to risk, Doctor."

Telek smiled sadly. "That, and you don't quite trust me yet."

"That is also a factor," Tuvok replied bluntly. He handed his phaser to Seven, squared his shoulders, and stepped forward.

And vanished.

They heard Tuvok moving about, his boots clicking on the floor, heard unseen objects gently clanking against one another. His disembodied voice carried clearly.

"Dr. R'Mor was correct. There are many tools and instruments here. I am not familiar with the functions of many of them. There are items which appear to be standard rations, and some fruit taken from Mr. Neelix's mess hall."

He reappeared as suddenly as he had disappeared. Seven scanned him with the tricorder. "The amount of dark matter in your tissue has increased by twenty-seven percent," she informed him. Tuvok merely nodded.

"Dr. R'Mor, it appears that—"

The dreadful sound of a weapon being fired interrupted Tuvok. Ramirez had half turned, and as Seven whirled, she saw him arch his back in agony and vanish.

She could see their quarry more plainly now. There was still a halo of shimmering matter surrounding the intruder, but it was recognizably a Romulan. Immediately after firing at Ramirez the Romulan clutched his side as if in great pain, but hatred and resolve filled his face. He lifted his weapon with an effort and pointed it straight at Seven.

Although Seven was the only one who could see the Romulan, they all had seen the disruptor fire. Before Seven could fire her own phaser, Kirby had fired first, moving to interpose his own body between the invisible Romulan and Seven. The Romulan collapsed without a sound, his peculiar halo disappearing, but Kirby staggered backward, his phaser falling from limp fingers.

Seven of Nine suddenly felt cold and her knees gave way. Johnson groaned and fell to her knees, clawing at her chest. Tuvok staggered, then he, too, collapsed. Only Telek R'Mor, who, at Tuvok's insistence, had stayed behind everyone else in the group, didn't seem immediately overcome.

"Telek R'Mor to sickbay! Emergency!"

Seven's vision swam. Surely that was what made the Romulan lying on the floor seem transparent in places. Most certainly that was what made the room fade away as she gave in to the weakness spreading through her body and tumbled forward.

* * *

Janeway's chest was tight with apprehension as she strode into sickbay, and the worried look on the Doctor's face did nothing to ease the knot.

"What the hell happened?" she demanded, looking at Seven, Tuvok, Kirby, Johnson, and a Romulan centurion all lying unconscious on the beds. Telek R'Mor was just sitting up as she came in.

"We found the stowaway, obviously," R'Mor told her. "He was indeed in Cargo Bay One. We confiscated his equipment, which I need to examine immediately. The centurion took us by surprise. He fired on one of your guards, killing him immediately. The young man," he nodded in Kirby's direction, "fired a phaser at him. The phaser blast dispersed the centurion's personal shield, and Seven, the guards, and, to a lesser extent, Commander Tuvok were all struck with heavy doses of dark matter."

"This matter is abominable," said the Doctor with the utmost solemnity, stepping through the forcefield that isolated his patients. "I doubt if we'll be able to save enough of the centurion for questioning. He's dying."

Janeway went to the edge of the forcefield and rubbed her eyes. Parts of the Romulan—his leg, his shoulder, a patch the size of her fist in the center of his chest—were . . . fading.

"My God," she breathed softly. "That's not a cloak, is it?"

"No," replied the Doctor. "Parts of his body are disappearing and reappearing. I've absolutely no idea where they are when they're gone. His entire

DNA sequence is rewriting itself even as we speak. He must have been in absolute torment for some time now. And what's even worse, I've detected the beginnings of similar activity in our people now as well."

"Doctor." Telek seemed to be barely restraining his rage. "Please let me examine the equipment we confiscated. The fact that there are Romulans—"

Janeway whirled. "Romulans? Plural?"

"I do not know for certain, but scout groups usually do not travel alone. There is mostly likely at least one other centurion aboard, Captain, and somewhere nearby you will find a cloaked vessel. The Romulans, their shields, and the vessel are by this point little more than clusters of mutated dark matter. Every moment we delay could be a moment too long. I beg you, give me access to the equipment. Let me discover what they were attempting to do!"

Janeway hesitated. By granting Telek access to the Romulan technology, they could be turning their fates over to him. But hadn't they done so already? Weren't they all in the same boat—or rather, on the same ship?

"Do it," she said.

Telek leaped from the bed and hastened to the Doctor's office. On the table were several pieces of equipment with which Janeway was utterly unfamiliar. They were all sleek and utilitarian looking, as coolly efficient as the beings who operated them.

As he slid into the chair, Telek gasped and reached for a long, cylindrical unit. It was glowing softly. At once he thumbed a control switch and the glow subsided. The face he turned to Janeway registered grim resignation.

"What is it?" asked Janeway.

"This is a homing beacon, to guide the fleet of cloaked vessels directly to *Voyager*. They have found us, Captain."

CHAPTER
10

"HOW MUCH TIME DO WE HAVE?" JANEWAY DEMANDED.

"It all depends on how long they have been aboard the vessel," Telek replied.

"It can't be very long," Janeway said. "We only just detected the transmission."

"They could have been here for several hours, perhaps even days, Captain," Telek replied. "The fact that they are here at all indicates that Chairman Kaleh and Lhiau have a good idea where we might be. The transmission serves to pinpoint our position. They will be upon us soon. We must leave this area of space at once!"

"We're not going anywhere until we've retrieved our warp core." Janeway tapped her badge. "Janeway to engineering. Status report."

"Torres here." B'Elanna's voice was faint and she

sounded tired, but at least she was at her station. "We've gotten the warp core back safely. Now all we have to do is install the thing."

"How long will that take?"

Over the link, Janeway heard a sputtering sound and a cry of pain. "Torres? What's happening?"

"Dammit!" Now Janeway's chief engineer sounded like her old, robust self. "A piece of diagnostic equipment just exploded in Carey's hands. Carey, you all right?"

A terrible suspicion began to seep through Janeway. Stepping in front of Telek, she began to tap the keys of the console and called up a schematic of the ship.

"Computer," she said, "isolate areas of largest concentrations of mutated dark matter aboard the vessel and in the surrounding area of space. Display all such areas in red."

In a heartbeat, the computer had responded, and there they were—three large, fluctuating, crimson areas that indicated huge masses of the deadly matter. One of them was right here in sickbay and was clearly the Romulan centurion they had captured. Another splash of scarlet was outside the ship, riding it almost like a parasite.

A third was in engineering.

Telek R'Mor caught her gaze and nodded. "It would make sense," he said. "We would do everything possible to disable the ship in preparation for boarding. Loss of lives—Romulan lives—would be avoided as much as possible."

"Shields, weapons, the warp drive—all would be

key areas in stopping the ship and rendering us unable to fight back," said Janeway. "And here we were, not trusting the computer, when all along it's been telling us exactly what's been happening. One centurion was going around the ship taking our weapons systems off-line and forcing us to eject the warp core. The other one was hiding in a quiet, out-of-the-way area to set up the homing beacon once his partner had accomplished his goal."

She slammed a fist down on the console. "Torres, listen to me. Get your people out of there now and shut down the area."

"Captain?"

"Do it!" cried Janeway. "Janeway to bridge. Chakotay, I've ordered a complete evacuation of engineering. Once everyone's out, I want you to flood the area with anesthezine and erect a level-ten forcefield. Go to Red Alert, and," she added, with a glance at Telek, "keep an eye out for approaching warbirds."

Rusan T'Kami huddled in a corner of engineering, too weak to even try to move and dodge the humans' bustle. It was all he could do to tap in the controls on his equipment and send out a burst of energy to make the instrument in the man's hand explode. He was certain these Federations would hear his labored breathing.

He wondered, idly, how much longer he would live.

The nausea had come first, a complete inability to keep anything in his stomach. For his companion Shurak, it had been headache and a parched mouth.

Later, they had both experienced intense pain, in bones, limbs, joints, skin, organs. Most alarming had been the times when one or the other had no recollection of the actions they had taken or of what had occurred.

There had been a tense moment, Shurak had told Rusan, when he feared they had been discovered. An inquisitive child had stumbled upon Shurak. Fortunately, she was half convinced he was something called a "ghost," and therefore not entirely real. Shurak had played upon her willingness to help him "cross over" and they had, for the time being, gone undetected by any less gullible adult crew members.

Eight they had been originally: eight stalwart members of the Romulan empire who had volunteered for the honor of chasing down the wayward *Voyager* and its traitorous passenger, Telek R'Mor. Four scoutships had gone through the wormhole to the Federation vessel's last recorded coordinates and departed in four different directions, each with the same set of orders: Find *Voyager.* Shurak and Rusan had been the fortunate pair who had done so.

With their incredible new cloaking abilities, it had been simplicity itself to slowly ease past the ship's shields and run parallel to it. They had beamed aboard undetected. Shurak's assignment had been to set up the homing beacon—a tricky task and one that required Shurak's delicate, experienced touch— while Rusan had gone about the business of meticulously disabling *Voyager*'s crucial systems.

Of course, a single starship, even one from twenty

years in the future, would not be able to withstand the onslaught of thirteen perfectly cloaked warbirds. But Jekri had been adamant: she wanted the ship intact. Better to win by subtle, unobtrusive means than out-and-out conflict. Maximum effect, minimal losses. Such had ever been the Romulan code.

Rusan had begun feeling ill from the moment he went aboard the scoutship, and had been growing progressively worse. He battled the pain valiantly, but he could remain at war with his own failing body only so long. He swallowed hard and tasted blood.

The female captain was now speaking through her commlink to the Klingon engineer. It was an effort to focus on the words, but Rusan managed.

"Torres, listen to me. Get your people out of there now and shut down the area."

"Captain?" The engineer seemed surprised.

"Do it!"

The engineer shrugged. "You heard the captain," she told her fellow crewmen. "We evacuate now. Carey, let's get you to sickbay."

Confused and irritated, the Federations did as they were told. They left, and the doors came slamming down. Rusan was as confused as they, but he was not about to waste such an opportunity. On legs that barely supported him, he staggered toward the controls. From here, he could—

A hissing sound reached his ears. Angrily, Rusan shook his head. Such specious sounds had occurred before. Once, he even heard his chairman lecturing him, which was of course impossible. He pressed on.

It was only when he realized that the room was fill-ing with gas that he understood what was going on.

Fear flooded him, not for his own personal safety—it was far too late for that, even if such a cowardly sentiment had crossed his mind—but fear that he would be discovered before the warbirds ar-rived, fear that all this effort, this agony, would be for nothing. Rusan had personally observed two Vulcans, one here in engineering and one on the bridge itself. They could force a mind-meld upon him, and in his weakened state he might not be able to resist.

The transporter beacon that would have beamed him and Shurak back aboard their small scoutship was in the cargo bay with Shurak. Rusan stumbled to the controls, frantically searching for a way to open the doors. There was none. The command to seal them had come from the bridge, not engineer-ing.

A broken cry of frustration escaped Rusan's lips, and he was immediately shamed by his weakness. Surely it was the strange illness ravaging his system that made him whimper like an infant. His mind was suddenly assaulted with images: his parents, his sib-lings, his mate, his chairman, Shurak, the alien faces of the Federations, the smirking, loathed visage of Lhiau.

The gas was having its effect. There was not much time if he was to succeed. He fell to the floor and barely had enough strength to remove the orange philotostan chip from his boot and swallow it.

"I die for Romulus," he whispered as the darkness came to claim him with long, greedy fingers.

"This one looks even worse than his friend," observed the Doctor, regarding the dead Romulan on the examination bed.

"Did the dark matter kill him?" asked Janeway.

"I'll need to perform a full autopsy." The door hissed open, and Torres and Carey entered. Carey's hands were little more than crisped flesh on bone, and his face was pale and sweating.

"That autopsy must take precedence," said Janeway, looking compassionately at Carey. "I'm sorry, but you'll have to wait."

"Captain—"

"Don't argue with me, Torres." Janeway's voice was hard. "Burned hands will be the least of your worries, Lieutenant Carey, if we don't figure out how to slow the progress of the dark matter. B'Elanna, start venting the anesthezine and get back to work on that warp core."

The door hissed again. Others entered, limping or sweating or whimpering. The Doctor sighed. "Everyone's getting sick," he said. "Can you at least send Ensign Paris down to lend me a hand?"

"I need him on the bridge," said Janeway. "I'll have Ensign Campbell assist you."

"She's the transporter officer!" complained the Doctor.

"She's got two good ears, she can learn." Janeway headed for the door. Telek's soft voice stopped her.

"Captain, I must . . . that is . . . is this autopsy really necessary?"

She stared at him in surprise. "You're a scientist, Telek. You should appreciate how vital this is."

He looked distressed. "We do not . . . it is not permitted for others to—"

A nearly crippling jolt of pain sliced through Janeway's skull. "Telek, I'd love to sit down with you over a cup of coffee and hash all this out in a civilized manner, but frankly I don't have time to discuss the niceties of your customs or your orders. Protocol goes out the airlock when lives are at stake, and one of those lives is your own. What the Doctor learns from autopsying the centurion could tell us how to stop this, maybe even reverse the effects. It could save your own people. I'm sorry it has to be this way, but those are my orders. Now. Return to your assignment of analyzing the equipment and keep me informed of your findings."

Telek opened his mouth as if to protest further, but Janeway kept going. He had been remarkably forthcoming, and she liked and respected him, but she was not going to waste a single second arguing over the treatment of a dead body while living, breathing people might be saved. The door closed behind her.

More bad news awaited her on the bridge. It was strange to see Chakotay at Tuvok's position. At least he, Harry, and Tom seemed to be more or less all right.

"Status report."

"Our weapons system is completely off-line, and our shields are down to less than ten percent. We're sitting ducks. One good phaser blast from those war-birds you warned us about and we're done for."

"Get teams on it immediately. We know now that it's not computer failures, it's sabotage. Any sign of those warbirds on long-range sensors?" She sat in her chair and winced. Suddenly, her skin felt as though it were on fire. Undoubtedly the nerve endings were now being attacked by the dark matter in her system.

"Negative, at least so far," said Kim. "Maybe we stopped the signal before it reached them."

"I don't think it's wise to underestimate the Romulans. Ever. They got it, all right. I fear Telek is right, that it's just a matter of time. Paris, continue en route to the Shepherd planet. We'll go on full impulse until B'Elanna can get that warp core back in place."

Good Lord, she was hurting. She clenched her teeth and willed the pain away. It ignored her and continued its white-hot burning. Sweat gathered at her hairline from the effort. Out of the corner of her eye, she saw Chakotay give her a concerned glance. He knew her far better than she liked, sometimes.

"We've found the two Romulans. What about their ship?"

"It's running a parallel course inside our shields. They must have approached us and gotten in by dropping to an extremely slow speed. We didn't even detect a blip from the computer," said Kim.

"And even if we had, we wouldn't have trusted it," said Janeway.

"The dark matter readings are extremely high," Kim continued. "It could be damaging our shield capabilities. Who knows what such a large concentration of it could do?"

"We've got to get rid of it. Janeway to sickbay. How's that autopsy coming?"

"Slowly and carefully," the Doctor replied. "Even more slowly when you interrupt."

"Learned anything?" Janeway ignored the EMH's sarcasm.

"Death was attributable to suicide. The centurion ingested a philotostan chip. The dark matter had spread throughout his system, but it had not yet built up fatal concentrations in the tissue. Not that we know how much concentration proves to be fatal yet. The dark matter has utterly ravaged all his systems. Death by massive organ failure was not far away, and it appears that any pain control systems were the first attacked. He suffered throughout the entire ordeal."

Janeway felt a pang of sorrow for the late centurion. He was an enemy, but no one deserved to die like that. She tightened her mouth. Nobody under her command was going to suffer the same fate, if she had anything to do with it.

"In your professional opinion, would it be hazardous for anyone infected with the dark matter to transport off the ship?" she asked, changing the subject.

"At this point, taking a shower might be hazardous for anyone infected with the dark matter," the Doctor replied tartly. "We simply don't know. I am operating, if you will pardon the pun, in the dark. Dr. R'Mor? Your advice?"

"Telek R'Mor here, Captain. You will recall that earlier I told you that dark matter reacts in a completely unpredictable manner. However, in our tests, centurions with dark-matter personal shielding, such as the ones in sickbay, had transported to and from vessels at short range with no ill effects. Of course," he added heavily, "that was before we knew that dark matter *had* ill effects."

"Would environmental suits delay any infection?" Janeway asked.

"I doubt it. Remember, the dark matter particles routinely pass easily through solid matter in their natural state. Even forcefields probably have only limited efficacy."

Janeway took a deep breath, thinking. "We'll have to take the risk. Chakotay, I want you to take Ensign Vorik and beam over to that scoutship. I'd send Torres, but we need her here right now. The ship needs to be disabled."

"Aye, Captain." Chakotay's face betrayed no hint of reluctance, despite the fact that no one knew for certain what would happen during beam-out. Janeway clung to the hope Telek had offered, that no ill effects had been observed when experiments had been conducted back in Romulan space.

Of course, that was before we knew that dark matter had ill effects . . . .

Janeway shook off the Romulan's ominous last comment. She couldn't afford to think about it. They all had jobs to do.

* * *

Chakotay nodded to Vorik as the Vulcan entered and lightly stepped onto the platform. He took a deep breath, ordered, "Energize," and hoped for the best.

He and Vorik materialized in the cargo area of a small scoutship. They'd checked to make sure that life-support was functional before they beamed over, of course; however, most of the lights were out and he was glad they'd brought wristlights. He shone a beam around. The console loomed up, dark and brooding like a hidden beast. What illumination came from various stations was blue and murky. He tapped his combadge. Ensign Vorik stepped forward and began to examine the console.

"Chakotay to bridge. We made it safely. Vorik's trying to shed some light on the subject, but—"

Suddenly the console sparked. Vorik grunted and stumbled backward, clutching his face.

Everything went black.

CHAPTER
11

"CHAKOTAY?"

Silence greeted Janeway. "Kim, what's going on?"

"All communications have been severed," the ops officer told her. "Massive interference. I'll keep trying on all frequencies."

"Do that. Janeway to R'Mor."

"R'Mor here," came the Romulan's voice.

"We've just lost all communications with the scoutship. I think they might be in trouble. I'm assuming you know your way around a scoutship?"

"It's been years since I piloted anything but the *Talvath,* and these ships do have a new design, but I certainly could be of assistance."

"Then get to the transporter room immediately," Janeway ordered, realizing just how far she was trusting this man from a race to which the Federation had long been hostile. She'd let him move freely about the ship, without a guard, had given him access to the computer system, and now was trusting that he would transport over to a vessel he knew better than they without attempting to escape.

But, as he had said when they first beamed him aboard, where could he go? He was a man out of time, twenty years and several thousand light-years from home. And he needed this cure as desperately as they did.

The unsettling thought that Telek might take the scoutship and use it to reach the Shepherd planet before they could crossed her mind, but she had to risk it. She had no idea what was going on aboard that scoutship. Chakotay and Vorik could be dying. The only one who could help them was Telek R'Mor.

The air was beginning to grow cold. It would be a while before the remaining air was exhausted, but Chakotay knew they had to get life-support reestablished as soon as possible. With only his wristlight for illumination, Chakotay stumbled toward the fallen figure of the Vulcan.

"Vorik! Are you all right?"

"That depends on the definition," said Vorik, his voice as smooth and cool as ever. Chakotay winced when he saw the face Vorik turned up to him. He was badly burned. "I can function; however, I am quite blind. I regret that I can no longer be of assistance."

Chakotay bit his lip. "Don't worry about it," he said. "I'll handle this just fine on my own."

Vorik's sharp ears must have detected the sound of Chakotay fumbling with the emergency medkit. "Commander, my situation is not life threatening. I have every reason to believe that the Doctor will be able to restore my eyesight and repair any dermal damage. I am assuming that we have lost life-support functions and perhaps other systems as well. That should be your first priority, and I should not hamper you in attending to it. I am presently, I fear, in your way. If you could assist me . . . I can walk, but—"

"Of course." Chakotay bent down and helped Vorik stumble to his feet. He walked him a few steps away and eased him down against a bulkhead.

At that moment, he heard the familiar sound of the transporter. He turned, phaser at the ready in case the person who materialized was foe instead of friend.

"Telek R'Mor," he said, suddenly wondering into which definition the Romulan fit.

"Captain Janeway sent me to see if I could be of help," said R'Mor. "What happened?"

He was already activating his tricorder as Chakotay described the series of events. With an ease born of familiarity, Telek stepped up to the console. He swore softly.

"Commander, assist me. We must hurry."

Chakotay moved in smoothly beside him. Speaking quickly, Telek instructed him on how to repair the communications grid. He himself concentrated on the life-support systems and lighting systems. Both of them were flat on their backs beneath the Romulan vessel's console. Chakotay was not unfamiliar with jury-rigging alien equipment, and he found that the Romulans were as logical as the Vulcans when it came to their setup. Everything was organized with an eye to efficiency, and it wasn't long before Chakotay got the knack of what went where. After that, it was just a question of opening panels and adjusting.

A soft whir came from where Telek was working, and a blue light filled the cabin. Chakotay's lungs heaved, and he gratefully gulped in a rush of fresh air. He hadn't realized how stale the air in the cabin had become. All around the ship, various consoles came to life with blinks of red, blue, and green lights.

"We have lights and life-support," grunted Telek as he edged out from beneath the console. "How are communications?"

"I haven't quite got it," replied Chakotay.

"I am not surprised. The dark matter is pervasive. I should have been able to get life-support back on in seconds. Try cross-connecting it with another system."

From where he lay beneath the console, Chakotay glimpsed Telek's long, booted legs when he craned his neck. He was in an utterly vulnerable situation. He smiled a little. Had it been six whole years since he had been someone the Federation distrusted? Above him, he could hear the tap-tapping of Telek's skilled fingers, then a sudden, sharp intake of breath.

"Commander Chakotay. The dark matter within this ship is making replicas of itself at an exponential rate. We have approximately eight minutes to get this ship as far away from *Voyager* as possible before it becomes pure dark matter."

For a second, Chakotay's heart seemed to stop. He recalled the "burst" of dark matter that had so debilitated Seven, Tuvok, Kirby, and Johnson. And he also realized that his life and that of Telek R'Mor were about to come to an untimely, but hopefully heroic, end.

"Take us out of here, Telek," he said, scooting out from under the console.

Telek tapped in the commands. Nothing. He let out an unexpected roar of frustration and pounded the console. "The engines are gone. They're not responding!"

"Then we'll have to reach *Voyager* somehow," Chakotay said firmly, hoping with all his heart that the dark matter interference would not prove such a thing impossible. Their combadges were dead, prevented from working by the dark matter that enveloped them like an invisible cloud. Their only hope was to get the ship's communications systems back on-line.

They exchanged glances and, as one, returned to a supine position beneath the console. They were in such close proximity that Chakotay could smell the Romulan's scent—not the same odor as humans, more coppery and metallic. Chakotay felt his own uniform clinging to his skin and knew that he, too, was sweating with apprehension.

"Mirror my movements," Telek said, and Chakotay did, connecting one beam of light with another, adjusting a coupling, tightening something here, removing a panel there.

The minutes ticked by. How much time had Telek given them? Eight minutes? How long ago had that been?

A sharp crack, and a harsh bark of surprised pleasure from Telek. "Done!" he cried, hastening out from under the console. He pounced on the controls. "R'Mor to *Voyager!*"

"Janeway here. Status report."

"Captain," said Chakotay, "we've got—" He looked at Telek.

"Three point seven minutes," said R'Mor.

"Three point seven minutes before this ship becomes a pure mass of mutated dark matter. It's got no power of its own. You've got to use a reverse tractor beam and get it as far away from the ship as you can. There's no telling what being that close to it will do to *Voyager.*"

"Understood. But I'm beaming you three over first."

"Captain, no! There's no—" Chakotay had been about to say "time for that now," but he dematerialized before the words left his lips.

He, Vorik, and Telek materialized on the bridge. Chakotay guided Vorik's hands to a railing and then immediately headed for tactical.

"Do it!" Janeway cried. At once, the massive tractor beam went into action. Steadily, but far too slowly for Chakotay's comfort, the beam pushed the green, now shimmering ship away from *Voyager.*

"More power," ordered Janeway.

"We're at maximum now," said Kim. For a long, agonizing moment, they all watched in silence as the tractor beam did its work. What would the scoutship do once it became pure dark matter? Explode? Would they survive?

The ship seemed to grow smaller and smaller. Chakotay glanced down at his controls.

"Fifteen seconds . . . ten . . . five . . ."

The scoutship seemed to twist violently, then simply disappeared. At once, the ship rocked, but easily, like a seafaring vessel of old on a large but gentle swell.

"We made it," breathed Paris.

"In a manner of speaking," said Kim glumly. "We've lost all weapons systems, all shields, and life-support is down thirty percent. The amount of dark matter now present in us and in the ship has jumped from fourteen to twenty-six percent."

"But we're still here, Ensign Kim," said Janeway. "We're still here. Bridge to engineering. How's that installation of the warp core coming?"

"We're close, Captain," said Torres. "But we're not there yet."

"Let me know the minute we have warp capability. In the meantime, Ensign Paris, proceed on course to the Shepherd planet. Ensign Vorik, what happened?"

"There was an exploding console," Vorik replied calmly. "Permission to go to sickbay."

"Granted. Ensign, Commander, Dr. R'Mor, that was good work. Doctor," she added, "you may join me here on the bridge. I imagine you'd like to be one of the first to see this Shepherd planet."

"Thank you, Captain," Telek replied, inclining his head. "I'm honored. But I find myself quite fatigued. If you have no immediate need of my services, I'll escort Ensign Vorik to sickbay and then retire to my quarters."

Janeway's eyes searched his. Then she nodded. "Of course, Doctor. We'll notify you the minute we are within sensor range of the planet."

Telek hadn't lied. He was tired, very tired. But he had no intention of resting. He first went to sickbay, to assist the brave ensign as well as to honor the dead and see if the other centurion was still clinging to life.

Even knowing what to expect, Telek winced as he saw the Doctor still engaged in the autopsy. The EMH glanced up and frowned as they entered. Telek helped Vorik onto a bed and the Doctor began to scan the Vulcan.

"Nothing a dermal regenerator won't repair. You're very lucky, Ensign Vorik," he said, picking up the aforementioned instrument and shining the warm red light on the ensign's burned eyes.

"How is the other centurion?" Telek asked, deliberately not looking at the body of the dead Romulan, graphically exposed in every possible manner.

"He's still alive, though I don't expect him to last much longer."

The door hissed open again and Naomi Wildman entered, her face wet with tears. The Doctor moved to block her view of the autopsy in progress.

"Naomi, what are you doing here? What's wrong?"

"Doctor, please let me see him," said the girl, her voice thick. "I can't believe I forgot him, but I just now remembered. Please."

"You remember the centurion? Your playmate?" Telek asked.

"Yes," she replied, "Mr. Ghost. At least, I thought he was a ghost. He was invisible."

"I'm afraid you can't speak with him, Naomi," said the Doctor gently. "He's very ill from the dark matter, and it could be transmitted to you. I can't let you past the forcefield."

Her face screwed up and turned red. "Oh, please, if he's dying, I especially need to see him!"

Telek felt unexpectedly moved by the girl's distress. He had hoped someday to see his daughter grow to become such a fine child, but . . . .

"At least let her approach the forcefield, Doctor," he urged.

"We don't even know how much, if any, good the forcefield does. She shouldn't even be in sickbay!" protested the Doctor.

"Naomi?"

The voice was rough, and so faint that Telek wasn't even sure he hadn't imagined it. But upon turning, he saw that the centurion was conscious and trying to lift his head. Even as Telek watched, parts of the Romulan faded in and out of sight.

The Doctor immediately went to him, causing a buzzing sound as he stepped through the forcefield that would have stopped Telek cold. He snapped open the tricorder and began to analyze the centurion.

"How do you feel?" the Doctor asked.

The Romulan ignored him, propping himself up on one elbow and trying to focus his gaze on Naomi. The girl went as close to the forcefield as she could, hiccuping through her tears.

"Mr. Ghost?"

Unbelievably, the Romulan smiled. "Yes, child."

"You're not dead."

"No," agreed the centurion, "but I will be soon." His gaze traveled to Telek R'Mor and his face hardened. "Get away from the traitor, Naomi," he hissed.

Telek, too, stepped as close to the forcefield as possible. "I am no traitor. I have always done what I felt was best for the Empire. We must not pollute the timeline."

The centurion swore. "You are the dung on our boots, R'Mor. We will smear you into the dust."

"There is something more important at stake now," said Telek. "The Empire has been used as a pawn. All of us, and especially you, my comrade. The illness from which you now suffer was caused by the personal dark-matter shield. It has turned your ship into mutated dark matter and is doing the same to you. Lhiau is using us, dangling the bait of galactic domination in front of us to make us dance to a tune he is piping. I, this child, this ship—we are all infected, just as you are."

"You are a liar," hissed the centurion, wincing in pain.

"I'm afraid he's telling the truth," said the Doctor.

"Please lie down and try to rest. The effort is further destroying your system."

"I do not care if I have one moment or ten left, Doctor. Speak you truly? The girl as well?"

"Everyone," confirmed the Doctor. "We are presently trying to contact the Shepherds and ask them for aid, in the hope that Lhiau is not typical of his species."

The Romulan lay back, exhausted from his feeble efforts, and frowned as he tried to make sense of everything he had been told.

Telek pressed his case, speaking quickly and urgently. "The cloaks on our thirteen warbirds will eventually consume them and their crew. No one who has contact with the dark matter will be safe. Please tell us, how many other ships did Chairman Kaleh dispatch to locate *Voyager?* If we can find them, we can perhaps rescue their crews, remove them from the direct influence of the ships and the personal shields."

Even as the words left his lips, Telek realized he had miscalculated. He had chosen the wrong argument. The Romulan, who had been listening, now tensed, and his face lost all expression save contempt.

"And this is how you think to trick me, traitor R'Mor. I shall not be fooled so easily. Liars all. The only innocents left in this universe are the children. Naomi?"

"Yes, Mr. Ghost," sobbed Naomi.

The centurion arched in pain. "I wish . . . to thank you."

"For what?"

"For helping me to pass on," whispered the dying Romulan. "It is good to see a young one again."

He smiled, and as the light of life left his eyes, Telek heard Naomi cry, "No!" She scurried to him and wrapped her arms around his waist, pressing her face into his abdomen. Gently, tentatively, Telek stroked her long hair and thought of his own daughter. He thought of the dreadful death the centurion had met, and of the thousands more who might even now be dying in such a fashion.

They had to reach the Shepherds and put an end to this nightmare. There was no alternative. Their battered bodies and disabled ship would somehow have to endure long enough to reach the planet.

Telek returned to his quarters, leaving the broken-hearted Naomi to the Doctor's care. Her image haunted him, as if she were a little ghost herself. The centurion had been right about one thing. In this troubled, dark universe where powerful aliens tricked the gullible into destroying themselves, the only innocents were indeed the children.

He sat down on the bed and reached for the padd he had left there earlier and began to write. Telek did not know if he would ever be granted the opportunity of the Right of Statement; he did not even know if he would survive long enough to finish writing it. Still, he had to try.

I stand before you as a condemned prisoner, he had begun, knowing exactly what verdict would be reached if he was even granted a trial. *But prisoner*

or no, I am a Romulan, and to that end I have pre-
pared this, my final statement. I do not question the
decision reached by my peers, nor is this a plea for a
different, more favorable verdict. Rather, I take this
opportunity to warn you of a terrible danger that is
encroaching upon us even as I speak.

It may seem peculiar that I use this last opportu-
nity for my voice to be heard to speak of scientific
matters. But hear me out, and perhaps this statement
may serve some greater purpose. I speak of dark
matter—and dark matters.

At some point in the crafting of the document, he
dozed. He was jolted into wakefulness by Captain
Janeway's voice.

"Janeway to Telek R'Mor. We've got the Shepherd planet on our long-range sensors. Please come
to the bridge at once."

CHAPTER

12

Janeway glanced up and threw Telek R'Mor a quick smile of greeting as he stepped onto the bridge. The smile ebbed slightly as she saw his expression. She knew the reason for it.

"My condolences on the deaths of your countrymen, Doctor," she said.

He nodded, accepting her sympathy. "Let us hope that this planet will be the key to preventing any more needless deaths," he replied.

"Engineering reports that we've got warp drive back," announced Kim, not bothering to hide his grin.

"Excellent. Mr. Paris, give us warp nine."

"Aye, Captain," Paris replied. The stars suddenly turned from small points of light to several long, white streaks as the ship sprang into warp. To Janeway, the minutes stretched on, but it was really only a brief time before Paris announced, "We've reached the planet, Captain."

Unable to hold back her enthusiasm, Janeway rose and walked down to the screen. The headache screamed for attention, but she ignored it. With any luck, all such ills and ones far worse would be cured quickly.

"Standard orbit, Ensign. On screen."

It filled the screen, a beautiful blue-green planet with large brown spots that marked eight clearly defined continents. Two small moons orbited it.

"Class-M," she breathed. They'd known that earlier, of course, but as far as Janeway was concerned, there were few things more beautiful than the image of a class-M planet on her viewscreen. One day— and she dared to hope that day would come soon— that would be Earth filling the screen, not an alien world.

"Report?"

"Standard class-M planet," said Harry. "Oxygen-nitrogen atmosphere. Good balance of plant and animal life. Two billion humanoid life-forms, level of technology comparable, in fact perhaps slightly superior to our own. There'll be no problems with the Prime Directive here."

"Thank God for that," Janeway said wryly. "I'd hate to come all this way and not be able to talk to anyone. Mr. Kim, open a channel."

"Hailing frequencies open, Captain."

"This is Captain Kathryn Janeway of the Federation *Starship Voyager*. We come on a peaceful mission, an attempt to make contact with a race of beings known as the Shepherds. We wish to discuss—"

Her words were cut off as the planet was suddenly engulfed in a brilliant white light. The ship rocked violently. Janeway flung up one hand to shield her eyes and gripped the arm of her chair with the other. When the radiance had faded, she blinked, then gaped.

The planet had disappeared.

"Tom, what the hell is going on? Did that . . . that light throw us out of orbit?"

"I don't know, Captain!" Tom was frantically scanning the controls. "According to the computer, we haven't been forced off course. We're continuing at standard orbit speed, but . . . but the planet's just not there!"

"Tom's right," confirmed Harry. "We're not the ones who have gone anywhere. We're moving along the same trajectory as we were. It's the planet. It simply vanished."

Janeway's headache was becoming almost unbearable, its slow red throb fueled by the adrenaline produced by this new, impossible development. Her hand crept to massage her temple despite herself.

"Any sign of Q activity? That would be just the sort of thing he'd do," growled Chakotay.

"Negative," said Kim. "It's just . . . *gone.*"

"This is not *possible!*" The words were torn from Telek's throat as he raced to join Janeway close to the screen, as if his simple, outraged presence could bring the vanished planet back. "Planets don't simply disappear!"

As he spoke, the screen again filled with the unbearably bright light. Again *Voyager* rocked. When her eyes had adjusted, Janeway could again see the planet, back in its proper position.

Except there was a horrible difference.

Before, the sixth planet in Sector 6837 had been a typical class-M planet. It was covered with oceans and rivers and clouds and continents, teeming with life. They could have beamed down and found themselves quite comfortable, in all likelihood standing on green, chlorophyll-fueled grass and gazing at a blue sky.

The planet before them now had no soft green-blue oceans. It had a swirling froth of gray and white instead. The continents had been utterly reshaped. Janeway didn't need Harry to sum it up for her, but he did.

"There have been earthquakes on every continent, hundreds of them," he was saying, speaking quickly and with a note of horror in his voice. "We've got tsunamis and volcanic activity in forty-seven different spots. The ozone layer has been completely obliterated, and the atmosphere is almost gone. I can't even believe it's still intact."

She knew the answer to the question before she voiced it, but it needed to be said. "Harry, any signs of life?"

A long pause. "No, Captain," said the ensign softly. "Not so much as a microbe."

The horrified silence stretched on. Janeway's mind simply couldn't grasp it. Two billion people gone, just like that, in the proverbial twinkling of an eye. What had happened? Who had done this?

Telek was the first to speak. "Ensign," he said to Kim in a rough voice, "are there any readings to indicate the presence of dark matter on the planet?"

Oh God, thought Janeway. *Can the dark matter be so virulent that it can descend like some kind of cloud and wipe out every living thing on an entire planet? Haul it off to who knows where, then toss it back again like a discarded toy?*

Harry looked shaken by the thought too. He tapped the consoles and located the requested information.

"Negative," he said. "There is absolutely no trace of dark matter either on or around the planet."

"What about the Shepherds?" asked Chakotay.

"The readings are still there," Kim replied.

"Then we're still going down," stated Janeway, lifting her chin a little in defiance of the disaster that had just happened. "Right now the planet's reappearance has us in an elliptical orbit. Tom, get us back into standard orbit."

"Captain—" began Chakotay.

"Harry, you said the atmosphere was almost gone. Could we survive down there?" Janeway barreled on over the protest of her first officer.

"Captain, there's seismic activity, there's no protection from radiation—"

"Answer my question, Ensign."

Glancing from Chakotay to Janeway, Kim replied, "Yes. Theoretically, we could survive down there for about two days, provided the seismic activity doesn't increase in frequency."

"It's far too dangerous!" cried Chakotay.

Janeway whirled on him. "We're all going to be as dead as everything down on that planet if we don't stop this dark matter from destroying us," Janeway said. "You were just on the ship. You know what it can do. It's killed two Romulans already, and by God, I'm not going to let this stuff get any of my crew if I can help it. The answers aren't here, Chakotay. They're down there, on that ghost planet, and I'm going to find them."

"Captain!" yelped Kim. "I've got a reading. There's a single life-sign on the planet. It wasn't there before, I'm certain of it."

He didn't need to say it, but they all thought it. It had just appeared, as the planet had just disappeared. Janeway's lips thinned. This could be no coincidence.

Who, or what, was the single life-form on that ghostlike planet?

The away team Janeway assembled consisted of herself, Telek R'Mor, Chakotay, Tom, and the Doctor. She'd left Kim in command and the rest of her senior staff was in sickbay. *And unless this mission is successful,* Janeway thought as she stepped onto the transporter platform, *they may never leave sickbay except in coffins.*

"Captain," said Ensign Campbell as Janeway entered the transporter room, "We've been having some erratic readings. I must tell you that I'm not at all certain about the transporter's ability to get you there and back safely."

"Perhaps we should take a shuttlecraft," suggested Chakotay.

Janeway considered it, then shook her head, stepping forward to check the transporter console for herself. "We're still within safety margins, though just barely. The shuttlecraft's as unknown as the transporter at this point. The dark matter is expanding at an exponential rate, and I don't want to waste time by taking the shuttlecraft. Find an open area near where the Shepherd activity was reported, Ensign. And keep us as far away from the shifting plates as you can. Let's take as few risks as possible."

Ensign Campbell looked unsure of herself and very young as she replied, "Aye, Captain."

Janeway patted her hand and gave her a smile. "I have every confidence in you, Lyssa."

She glanced around at her away team, making sure everyone had phasers at the ready. Everything that had once lived on the ghost planet might be dead now, but the appearance of a lone life-form and their own sensor readings indicated that the atmosphere was indeed, as Kim had reported, adequate. They might be the only ones breathing down there, but at least they'd be able to do so. For a while, at any rate.

"Brace yourselves," she told them. They knew what she meant.

And yet, and yet, nothing could prepare her or her crew for the utter bleakness and horror of the sight that met their eyes once they materialized on the ghost planet, in what had clearly been a large, open market square of some kind. Large paving stones had broken into jumbled shards from the activity, and here and there Janeway saw the enormous stone shapes of toppled statuary. None of the small buildings had survived intact, and even now, she imagined she could feel the unhappy planet rumbling beneath her feet, waiting to vent its rage at its impossible abduction with violent eruptions. The air was thin, but breathable. Barely. Kim had been right. They couldn't tarry here long.

She looked down with compassion at the bodies that were strewn everywhere. The heavyset, pale-purple-skinned humanoids who had moments ago been healthy, active beings lay where they had fallen. The deaths had obviously occurred instantaneously, literally from one step to the next. There was no sign of fear on the lumpy faces or in the postures of the corpses. Even those who were pinned beneath debris and rubble didn't appear to have struggled to escape.

For that brief mercy, the mercy of not realizing what was happening, Janeway was grateful. She was not unfamiliar with the horrors of war and, even in this day and age, natural disaster. But that did not mean she had grown used to them. She hoped she never would. Slowly, respectfully, she knelt and pressed her fingers to the throat of one of the beings.

"The flesh is still warm," she said, sorrow tingeing her voice.

The Doctor had his tricorder out. "It appears that

they suffered immediate total system failure. Everything just stopped."

"They literally fell dead in their tracks," said Paris softly. Out of the corner of her eye, Janeway saw him suppress a shudder and turn away a little too quickly.

"What killed them?" she asked the Doctor, rising.

"I wouldn't be able to say without a full autopsy. But there are no elevated levels of adrenaline. They didn't suffer at all, Captain."

She nodded her acknowledgment, took a deep breath, and stood up straighter. "Alive one second, dead the next . . . But there's no time to worry about the dead. I'm more interested in finding that single life-form we detected on board—and finding the Shepherds. Telek?"

"They are here, Captain." He alone, of all of them, seemed unmoved by the plight of the planet. Janeway didn't think him callous; she'd gotten to know him better than that. He was simply focused, and she supposed she couldn't blame him. He had been the one to unwittingly unleash the dark matter on an unsuspecting vessel, and he was clearly driven to undo the damage he had inadvertently wrought.

"The readings are strongest right . . . there." Telek turned and pointed, and Janeway's heart sank.

His long, slim finger indicated the top of a range of mountains that surrounded the city in which they stood. There was still snow on the highest peaks. The sky against which they were silhouetted was ominously dark. The weather patterns here could be depended on to be completely undependable.

Janeway briefly entertained the idea of contacting the ship and having Lyssa Campbell transport them directly to the site, but banished the idea immediately. Tempting as it was, it was far too risky. Had the transporter been operating at peak efficiency, it would have been child's play, but now it was unpredictable.

They could materialize on an outcropping that might choose that moment to give way beneath their feet, or they might trigger an avalanche. And there was a damn good chance that the coordinates might be just a little off and they'd materialize inside the rocks instead of on them.

They were going to have to do it the old-fashioned way. There were going to have to climb up on their own.

Her eyes met Chakotay's. "The mountain is *not* coming to Mohammed this time," she said.

He gave her a wry grin as he touched his combadge. "Chakotay to bridge. We've just run into our first obstacle. The Shepherds have ensconced themselves on top of a mountain range.

"Tom, you're our resident mountain goat. What will we need?"

Tom took a deep breath and blew it out. "What won't we need? Plenty of water, gloves, climbing boots, self-driving pitons, hooks, several lengths of rope, crampons, headgear, wristlights in case that damned signal is emanating from a cave, rappel brake . . . ."

While Paris, Chakotay, and Telek discussed the

practicalities of getting the away team up the mountain, Janeway turned to the Doctor.

"That's half of why we're here. What do you have on the other life-sign, Doctor?"

He didn't answer immediately, and his mouth twisted in an expression of pique. "Curse this dark matter," he grumbled. "I thought that was what was going on when we were aboard the ship, and apparently, either it's infected our equipment, or what happened to the planet is rendering my readings incorrect. Look," he added, petulantly, and shoved the tricorder at her.

Janeway sighed. "We are simply not going to get a break, are we?" she said, rhetorically.

She'd not had the chance to examine the life-form readings herself before leaving *Voyager*, but she knew that Kim had said there was something odd about it. And there was.

It was all backwards. Scrambled, unbalanced. As if she were Naomi and not capable of deciphering it herself, the Doctor edged closer. Unable to resist, he extended a finger and tapped angrily at the readings that were almost literally under his captain's nose.

"Look at this, just look at it! The DNA sequence is completely backwards, there's a high concentration of uracil *and* thymine, adenine is paired with cytosine instead of guanine, the gene sequence is just all wrong . . . Bah! How can I function properly without correct, reliable information? I cannot make bricks without straw!"

Suddenly Janeway chuckled. The chuckle blossomed into a laugh. The Doctor frowned at her. "What's so funny?"

"Oh, Doctor," said Janeway, wiping at the tears of mirth that sprang to her eyes, "I think this is something that you'll never be able to understand fully. This whole situation is so absurd, you've just got to laugh. Matter that's not matter as we know it is devastating our bodies and our ship. Some Romulans want to trap us, others want to help us, and none of them is from our time. The Shepherds are the ones who are causing all of this, and yet it's precisely the Shepherds to whom we're turning for help. A planet just blips in and out of existence, and the only living thing on it can't possibly be alive according to your readings. You've got to admit," she said, playfully shoving the tricorder into his chest, "it's pretty funny."

He followed her as she walked back to the group. "I see nothing at all humorous in our situation!"

"Come on, Doctor," Janeway said, "laughter is the best medicine."

He sniffed. "Oh," he said, sarcasm dripping from the words, "*there's* a line I haven't heard before."

Sobering, Janeway changed the subject. "Regardless of what your tricorder is saying, everything does point to a life-form reading on the planet. Telek, keep monitoring the Shepherd activity. I want to know if there's any kind of change: if it changes location, changes to a different frequency, grows stronger or weaker, anything. Is that understood?"

"Yes, Captain."

"Paris, Chakotay, you two stay here and get us ready for . . ." She paused, glanced up at the mountain and the churning black skies beyond it, and grimaced. "For that. Doctor, you and I are going to find this strange being and see if we can't get some answers."

The two of them followed the trail the bizarre readings indicated. Once, the planet trembled from aftershocks. Janeway immediately checked in with her crew, and luckily no one was injured.

Janeway wasn't sure what to expect. There was nothing to indicate that this might be one of the Shepherds; the readings were entirely different.

But what was it? A new life-form, born the moment the rest of this ghost planet died? The killer, come to gloat about his cruel victory? She knew she shouldn't be speculating. She had nothing to go on.

The Doctor was silent, save for a few muttered complaints against the equipment. Because there was no protective ozone layer, the grass beneath their feet was already turning brown and crackly. Dust stirred with their footfalls. Their path led them out of the demolished city of the newly dead and into the soft, rolling shapes of the foothills.

"The readings are getting stronger," the Doctor said.

"Approximate mass size?"

"The tricorder refuses to cooperate," growled the Doctor, whapping the offending instrument with his hand. Janeway had to smile. "Ah, there we are. Fifty-five kilograms, one hundred sixty-four centimeters tall."

"Humanoid?"

"The measurements fit, but it could be anything. Especially if any of these readings are actually accurate." He paused. "Six meters up ahead," he said in a voice barely above a whisper. "Behind that pile of boulders."

Janeway drew her phaser. She locked gazes with the Doctor and nodded.

"Come out from behind the rocks," she ordered in a clear voice that carried. "We are armed and we will defend ourselves if necessary."

There was no response at first. Then Janeway heard a heavy, very human-sounding sigh. "You won't need any weapons," came a soft, female voice.

The being rose from where she had been sitting behind the boulders. She was the most beautiful young woman Janeway had ever seen, and her eyes held a world of pain.

185

CHAPTER

13

PARIS WAS NOT IN THE MOOD FOR MOUNTAIN CLIMB-
ing, and by that indication alone, he knew he was
really ill. The others had talked about his displays of
"paranoia," but his thoughts and reactions always
seemed rational to him. He couldn't understand what
they were talking about.

But this . . . Tom remembered loving the exhilara-
tion of a good climb. He knew that once he'd have
tackled this challenge with a grin. Now, all he wanted
to do was go back to the ship and sit in his quarters,
seeing no one, not even B'Elanna, and doing nothing.
And that's how he knew that he was indeed as sick
from the dark matter infection as he could possibly be.

"Ready to beam down equipment," came Lyssa's
voice on his combadge.

"Okay," he told her.

Two pairs of hiking boots and a backpack materialized a meter in the air and fell to the dry earth with a thunk. A wristlight and three bottles of water materialized inside the earth, only partially visible.

Tom swallowed hard. Behind him, Chakotay cleared his throat.

"That could have been us," said Paris softly.

"Seems like the captain was right in not choosing to beam us directly to the Shepherd's readings," said Chakotay in a calm voice, as if nothing untoward had happened.

Chakotay moved forward and began to gather the equipment. After a moment, Tom joined him, moving slowly. Unspoken were the words, *What if the Shepherds aren't really here, or won't help us? How much longer will this planet remain stable? How will we return to* Voyager, *and what kind of nightmare will we be returning to?*

The female was humanoid, with a cascade of thick, light blue hair and eyes of a deeper sapphire shade. Her pale skin, too, had a blue luster to it, like a pearl in twilight shadow. She wore what appeared to be a uniform not unlike Starfleet's, a standard one-piece garment with bold, geometric designs. Her eyes were puffy and swollen, as if she had been crying.

"Who are you?" demanded Janeway, her caution not diminished by the flicker of pity she felt for this young woman.

"My name is Shamraa Khala Remilkansuur," she replied.

"Is this your planet?"

The woman swallowed. Her eyes grew shiny. "No," she said.

"Are you one of the Shepherds?"

She looked puzzled and shook her head. "I don't know that term."

"Are you responsible for what happened here?"

"No!" she cried, outraged. "I don't know what happened, and I don't know how I—" The woman paused. "Did you bring me here?"

"No," Janeway replied, echoing the woman's earlier negatives and lowering the phaser. "But I do have a lot of questions for you, Shamraa."

A ghost of a smile touched the woman's lips. "Shamraa is a title, a ranking. My—" There was a quick series of liquid sounds before the translator caught up with the woman's speech. "My speaking-with name is Khala."

Janeway's combadge chirped. "Chakotay to Janeway."

"Go ahead, Commander."

"The equipment has been transported down—well, most of it, anyway."

"What do you mean?"

"There was a malfunction. Some of the gear materialized in the air, some inside the soil. Good call, Captain."

Janeway took a deep breath. "We're on our way. Janeway out." Her blue eyes took in Khala from head to toe. "We don't know if you're a friend or a foe, Shamraa Khala. But you're coming with us until we find out. Doctor, how are those crazy readings doing?"

His eyes fastened on his tricorder, the Doctor shook his head slowly. "I don't know what's going on, Captain. I'd like to get our new acquaintance up to sickbay and do a full scan on her."

"Believe me," replied Janeway with a hint of grim humor, "I'd love it if we could get her up to sickbay, but unless we find the Shepherds, I don't think any of us is going anywhere. Come on, Doctor. Let's rejoin the others and prepare for a good long hike."

Khala was willing, almost eager, to go along with the Doctor and Janeway. Janeway didn't blame her. If what she said was true, then she had somehow been brought here, to a dead but still dangerous planet, against her will and with no knowledge as to why. Anybody's presence, as long as it was not hostile, would be welcome, even comforting, after an ordeal like that. As they began walking back toward the rest of the away team, Janeway put away her phaser. There were more pressing matters than training a phaser on a nonaggressive, confused, and frightened young woman.

"I see you found the life-form," said Chakotay as Janeway and the Doctor approached with Khala. Thunder rumbled in the distance. Chakotay glanced at his captain questioningly.

"This is Khala. She claims that she was taken from her planet and suddenly appeared here, apparently at the same time the planet disappeared."

Chakotay scrutinized Khala, who stood straight and tall under his examination. Finally he nodded and offered her a drink from one of the few remaining water bottles.

"Thank you," Khala said, reaching eagerly for the bottle.

"Hey, go easy on that," said Paris harshly. "This is all we've got and we don't know how long this is going to take."

"I'm sorry," Khala apologized, wiping her mouth.

Janeway turned and regarded the mountain. "Let's go."

At first, it really was just a hike, albeit a challenging one. Chakotay actually enjoyed the workout. He kept a close eye on Khala, but she matched their pace and seemed completely without a desire to escape. Perhaps she was telling the truth after all.

They made good time for the first few hours. The storms that threatened constantly did not break, though the wind picked up. The Doctor monitored their physical conditions. During a break, Telek took out his tricorder and examined the readings.

"The signal has not moved," Telek said. "The Shepherds must be waiting for us. I cannot imagine that they have not detected our advance."

"I hope that's good news," Janeway said, panting. She wiped her wet brow with the back of her gloved hand and gulped at their dwindling supply of water.

"Once we meet them, Captain," Telek said, "we will certainly know one way or the other."

Janeway removed her own tricorder and examined it. "Let's pick up the pace if we can, gentlemen. This planet isn't getting any calmer."

Despite her admonition, the hours crawled by, and the trek became far less of a pleasant exercise and more of a grueling challenge. Their stops became more frequent, and the water level in the bottles dropped steadily.

When what passed for a trail finally petered out and they stood facing a sheer wall of stone, they all stood and stared for a long moment. Wordlessly Paris stepped forward and drove the first few self-setting pitons while everyone else rummaged through their packs and donned harnesses. With a clanging sound, the pitons slammed into place.

"Doctor, you first," said Chakotay. If the seemingly omnipresent dark matter was in the pitons, the Doctor's weight would test them without risking a human life. He glared at Chakotay, then, muttering under his breath, stepped forward and threaded his rope, attaching it securely to his harness.

"I do have pain sensors in my program, you know," he told them as he scaled the cliff face. "It lets me know when I am, as Seven would put it, damaged." He had reached the highest piton Paris had set and began driving some of his own to continue the climb.

"Yes, Doctor," said Janeway, "but you're a bit easier to repair than we are."

"I don't understand," said Khala, who had for the most part been silent on this trip. "He is incapable of being injured?"

"He's a hologram," said Chakotay. "He can go first and make sure the pitons are set properly. If they give way and he falls, he won't be hurt."

"That's a matter of perspective, Commander," came the Doctor's voice from high above them. They had to crane their necks to see him. " 'Hurt' is a relative term."

"He's almost there," said Janeway. They heard and saw two more pitons being driven into the cliff, then the Doctor disappeared momentarily. A few seconds later, he peered down at them, scowling.

"It's safe to come out now," he said, unfastening his harness. "Khala, you may use mine." Khala gave him a grateful smile.

Chakotay went next, making sure the rope was tied to his harness, then tossing up the end to the Doctor. The climb, thanks to the Doctor's setting of the pitons, was fairly easy. Chakotay had watched the Doctor closely and made a mental note of where toeholds could be found. Still, when the Doctor helped him onto the ledge and he peered down at the rest of his crewmates, Chakotay was just as glad he'd had the safety harness on.

Khala went next, her lithe, strong body having no trouble negotiating the rocky surface. Then came Telek, looking uneasy and more than a little nervous. He did not seem particularly unfit, but Chakotay surmised that regular rigorous workouts such as mountain climbing were not part of the scientist's daily routine.

He had almost made it when the last piton gave way and he lost his footing. Gasping, Telek reached for Chakotay's hand. The sudden, frightened gesture made him lose his balance and he fell, hurtling downward for only a meter or two before the rope securely fastened to his harness halted him.

Dangling from the rope, the Romulan swung back and forth. "There's an outcropping about a meter to your left. Try to grasp it!" Chakotay cried. Grunting, Telek reached and missed, swinging past the jagged, jutting rock, then returning. He clasped it firmly on the second try and Chakotay breathed a sigh of relief.

They pulled him to safety, and Telek did his best to aid them by pulling himself up on what finger-holds he could reach. When they hauled him over the edge, their fingers clutching his harness, Telek was breathing heavily and trembling.

Chakotay felt a rush of sympathy, but the expression on the Romulan's face turned the commander's emotions to respectful amusement. Telek's face was flushed and his eyes very bright.

"Exhilarating!" he managed, gasping for breath. "Walking on the edge of terror and a sort of giddy joy—I've never experienced anything like it!"

"If you stay with us, Dr. R'Mor, it'll become second nature," came Janeway's voice, floating up to them.

Chakotay sobered at once. "Captain, double-check your harness. The pitons are obviously not as secure as we'd like."

Janeway did so, tightening some buckles and tugging on it to make sure it held, then she began to ascend. Slender and strong, she made it look easy. Chakotay watched in admiration.

"Chakotay." The Doctor's's voice was taut. "The rope—"

Instantly alert, Chakotay followed the Doctor's gaze and his gut clenched. The constant activity had begun to fray the rope.

"We've only used it for four people," he said softly to the Doctor. "It shouldn't show any signs of wear." Their eyes met, and neither of them had to say it. The dark matter inside the rope's molecules was making it weaker.

Chakotay leaned forward, intending to grab the rope below the frayed point. At that instant, he heard a scrabbling sound. One of the pitons had given way beneath his captain's weight, slight though it was. Janeway grunted in startlement and turned her pale, dusty face up to his. She wore an expression of alarm, but not fear.

She was almost within reach. "Tom, take the rope," Chakotay ordered. He threw himself down onto the rocky ledge and edged forward as far as he could, reaching his hands out to his captain.

Janeway was hanging on with one hand, her body swaying several meters from the rocks below. Not realizing what was happening with the rope, she brought her other hand up toward it, to pull herself up with it.

Chakotay watched the right hand come up, as if in slow motion, the strong, capable fingers close slowly around the rope, thinking it to be a source of safety. He tried to cry out, to move forward, but he couldn't do it fast enough.

The rope broke with a snap just as Chakotay surged forward. He felt himself slipping, felt three sets of hands seize his legs and barely stop him from falling, felt the rough surface of the rock fraying his harness and tearing his uniform.

He gazed into his captain's blue eyes, wide with disbelief, and prayed with all his heart.

His hands closed over her wrist. The sudden pull of the weight of her body sent pebbles and earth slipping off the ledge and he felt himself slip farther down. The edge of the rock dug painfully into his abdomen.

But he had her. He had her.

"Pull us up," Chakotay grunted, not sure if he could even be heard. Hands seized his uniform and shoulders and hauled him back from the edge. He gripped Janeway's slender wrists with all his strength, refusing to let go. More scrambling, more dust kicked up, then suddenly she was lying on top of him gasping, and Chakotay let go of her wrists to clasp her to him for a brief, precious second.

She was pale, but managed a reassuring smile. "Thank you," she said, softly. Then, more loudly and cheerily, "Good thing my senior staff likes to keep in good shape."

"Your wrists are sprained," said the Doctor, running his tricorder over her hands.

"I'll take sprained wrists in exchange for an intact body any day," his captain replied. "No, don't. We don't have time," she said as the Doctor fished around in his pack for his instruments. "If we get the Shepherds on our side, we'll have plenty of time to treat any minor injuries. And if we don't, it won't matter. Everyone else all right?"

They nodded, concern for her plain on their faces. Chakotay wished his didn't reveal so much. His abdomen burned, and he realized his uniform was torn and bloody. He had barely noticed the pain in his concern for his captain. Now it rushed over him and as he touched his belly, it was hard not to wince. But if Janeway wasn't willing to take the time to treat her painful wrists, he could let his abraded abdomen go for the time being as well.

Janeway nodded, then briskly rose to her feet.

The rest of the way was still difficult, but there were no more sheer walls. No one said anything, but Chakotay imagined they were all as relieved as he was. There weren't enough pitons left to scale any more cliff faces, and they had just had it made very plain that the remaining pitons could not be trusted.

He winced a little as Janeway, thinking herself unobserved, removed her climbing gloves and hissed softly with pain. Her hands were white, save for the angry red bands around her wrists. Chakotay could even make out the marks of his individual fingers. He regretted having to hang on so hard, but Janeway had been right. The sprains would heal. A smashed body, broken on the rocks, would not.

He suppressed a shudder and turned away from the image. "Any change in the signal?" he asked Telek, trying to focus on something else.

Telek looked up at him, annoyed. "I said I would

notify the captain if there was any change. There has not been."

A sudden swell of anger rose in Chakotay and he had an almost overwhelming urge to beat the smug Romulan's face into a green, bloody pulp. He quelled it, but the struggle with his own emotions made sweat break out on his dark face.

This was his burden to bear, he had realized that early on. Even before his encounter with Coyote, with the dark, slippery, Trickster part of his innermost self, he had known. This was how the dark matter growing inside his body was affecting him. It was awful, this loss of control, as if his own mind was a panther he commanded by sheer brute will, a dangerous creature that could, at any moment, slip from that tenuous control to spring on his companions, his friends, as Coyote had sprung on him. Chakotay was willing to fight, willing to die or even kill, for a worthy cause.

Anger was not such a cause.

They pressed on in grim silence. The temperature was falling, and the wind now had a voice, howling from time to time. The skies were black, and even the sun's light was beginning to dim. The smoke belched forth by the volcanoes was doing a good job of providing a black curtain. The red rocks were dusted with snow and soot, turning slick and treacherous beneath their booted feet. The snow grew deeper, and finally they found themselves slogging through half-meter-deep drifts. Breathing became harder, the air thinner.

Chakotay ran a tricorder over the snow. There was nothing harmful in it. In fact, there was almost nothing in it at all—no microscopic organisms, nothing. Other than the ash that dusted the tops of the drifts, it was pure water.

"No need to watch the water supply any more," he said to Janeway, who had come to stand beside him. "The snow is perfectly safe."

She didn't answer, merely knelt and began to scoop white snow into the open mouth of her water bottle. Everyone else did the same.

"Food is going to be another matter," said Chakotay. "We're burning a lot of calories, more than we expected. Since the transporter isn't working properly, we shouldn't request any more supplies. Who knows what would be in the food at this point. If we have to go much longer, we—"

"We will not," Telek R'Mor interrupted. His face was bright with excitement. He pointed upward. "They are there—in that cave."

Janeway glanced at Telek's tricorder. "Provided the equipment isn't malfunctioning, then Telek's right. Everyone, listen. We're almost at the end of our journey. Check your phasers and wristlights. We're going in."

The way up to the cavern was not difficult, though the snow and slippery rocks made for slow, careful going. At the entrance of the cavern, Janeway nodded silently. Everyone grasped phasers and waited for the command.

Janeway and Chakotay went first, followed by

Telek R'Mor and Paris. The Doctor and Khala brought up the rear.

It was cold in the cave, but after the harsh wind it felt almost warm. At first they saw nothing. "Hello?" Janeway called. Her voice echoed mockingly. She shrugged.

"Maybe they wanted us to knock first," Chakotay said.

She smiled fleetingly at that, but quickly grew sober. "Fan out, everyone. Telek, where's the signal coming from?"

"Straight ahead, about another twenty meters," the Romulan replied.

"Then that's where we go."

No sooner had the words left her lips than the earth shifted. Chakotay lost his footing almost at once and hit the stone floor with a grunt. Instinctively, he covered his head and felt bits of rock and sand strike his body. The rumbling sound filled his ears and for a brief moment, he was certain that he was about to join his ancestors. He could almost see Kolopak standing in front of him, extending a hand to help him along.

After an eternity that in reality lasted less than half a minute, the quake stopped. Rocks still fell, their crashing noises echoing. Chakotay was breathing heavily and felt bruised and battered. Experimentally, he tried to move and found that everything still worked.

Faint flashes of light came from here and there. Someone's wristlight was still working, then.

"Is everyone all right?" Janeway shone the light

on her own face, casting her pleasant features into a caricature of angles and shadows, showing her crew that she was uninjured. "Chakotay?"

"I'm fine," he said. Others were moving now, their lights shining about. It seemed as though everyone had made it through without serious injury, though Tom was cradling his arm. His dust-covered face looked pale to Chakotay, and a second glance showed him a jagged tear in Tom's uniform and skin through which the whiteness of bone peeked.

"Let me see that," said the Doctor. While he tended to Paris's arm, everyone else rose and stretched, brushing debris off their bodies.

Chakotay went to Paris. "That looks bad," he said.

"Oh, thanks, Chakotay, that helps," said Paris through clenched teeth. The Doctor rocked back on his heels.

"I've done the best I could with the medkit, but I'd like to get him to sickbay as soon as possible," the Doctor told Janeway, who had moved to stand beside him. He finished wrapping Tom's arm, then rose.

Janeway extended a hand to the ensign. "How are you, Tom? Can you continue with us?"

"I sure don't want to miss the big finish after all this," said Tom, trying to smile but grimacing instead from the pain.

Janeway smiled and squeezed his shoulder reassuringly. "We'll get you a front-row seat. Let's keep going." Nobody bothered to say that, with their exit blocked by kilotons of stone, the only direction was forward.

Slowly, watching their steps, the away team moved forward and down. The signal might be straight ahead, but their path was undulating and winding, leading them deeper into the heart of the mountain.

"Only a few yards now," said Telek, a telltale excitement creeping into his normally evenly modulated voice. "I don't understand why they're so still. They must be waiting to greet us formally."

"Or kill us," said Janeway. "We've got to be ready for that possibility."

He nodded, his eyes on the tricorder. "The area opens up into a cavern," he said. "Right around the corner."

"Phasers at the ready," ordered the captain. She took a deep breath, nodded to Chakotay, and stepped forward.

A soft, purple illumination flooded the cavern. The bright white light of their wristlights seemed a garish intrusion. Stalactites and stalagmites decorated the floor and ceiling, and the violet glow turned their white, milky forms to glowing icicles. There was a clear area from which no stalagmite thrust upward, but there was no sign of any lifeform.

The light came from a large, floating sphere. A soft, pleasant hum registered in Chakotay's ears. It was almost hypnotic. He felt better here, in a strange place confronted by possibly hostile alien technology, than he had on *Voyager* for weeks.

"They're not here." Telek's voice was bitter with

disappointment. "All along, I've been tracking their technology, not them!"

"Don't despair yet, Doctor," said Janeway. She moved forward cautiously. The purple light was reflected in her eyes. "Chakotay, what have you got?"

"Oh." Chakotay blushed. He'd been so caught up in the ethereal beauty of the levitating sphere that he'd completely forgotten to take out his tricorder. He did so quickly and scanned its readings. "It's like no technology I've ever seen. There's some kind of energy animating the sphere, coming from inside, but I don't know how to explain it. I can't even estimate its function."

"Telek? Any thoughts?"

The Romulan struggled, visibly wrestling with his disappointment. "This appears to be similar to the apparatus they gave us to manipulate dark matter. My method of tracking down the Shepherds was never exact, Captain. I knew how to look for signs of their activity. I incorrectly assumed that this signified their presence, not simply a piece of their technology. I apologize for our failure."

"It's ancient, that's for sure," said Chakotay. "This sphere has been here for hundreds of thousands of years. Its energy is only detectable on the very narrow, precise band that Telek gave us. I'd say it's unlikely that the inhabitants of this planet were even aware it was here."

Janeway nodded thoughtfully. She stepped closer and regarded the hovering purple orb from a distance of only a few centimeters.

"They didn't make it easy for anyone to find it," she said softly. "That very narrow band, hidden away in this cave—only a select few would even know to come looking for it."

"What are you getting at?" asked Chakotay.

Her blue eyes met his. "This was left here to be found, Chakotay. Found by someone who knew enough to track it down. I'm betting that we haven't failed after all, Telek. I think this is a way to contact the Shepherds."

"But how?" asked Telek.

A slow, soft smile lit up Janeway's features. "There's only one way to find out. We guess."

And she stepped up and placed her hand on the purple sphere.

Light spread out, flooding the room with violet brightness. Chakotay shut his eyes against the illumination. Janeway didn't appear harmed at all, and she kept her hand atop the smooth surface of the sphere. Inside the sphere, something began to swirl. It looked like smoke, curling and twining, but it gradually began to take on form and solidity. For a wild second, it reminded Chakotay of a fetus, glimpsed inside its mother's womb. But a heartbeat later it had changed, growing and pressing against the confines of the orb.

Janeway backed away just as the orb shattered with a musical tinkling sound. Tiny crystalline prisms turned every shade of the rainbow and then vanished.

The light dimmed to a comfortable level. Bathed in that soft radiance stood an old woman. Chakotay gaped. It looked like Karanuk, an elder of his tribe who he knew had died many years ago. Her brown eyes bored into his and her wrinkled face wrinkled still further in a smile.

"Grandma?" he heard Paris say. Simultaneously Janeway breathed, "Aunt Elyssa—it's not possible!" Telek, too, reacted as if he recognized the woman, and even Khala seemed startled. Alone of them all, the Doctor seemed not to know her.

Abruptly Chakotay realized that the being—the Shepherd, for that was who it must be—appeared different to each of them. But it—she—was clearly female.

"I am Tialin of the Shepherds," said the woman in Elder Karanuk's frail but somehow compelling voice. "You need my help. And we need yours."

CHAPTER

14

"I DON'T UNDERSTAND," SAID JANEWAY. "YOU NEED *OUR* help?"

Tialin smiled. Damn, but she looked like Elder Karanuk. "Please sit and be comfortable," she said, and at once five chairs that might have been taken directly from *Voyager* appeared. Janeway didn't make a move, and her crew followed her example.

Tialin sighed. "I suppose after your encounter with Lhiau I can understand your suspicion. Still, this may take some time. I suggest you make yourselves at home."

They still did not move. With a wave of her hand, Tialin created a seat for herself. Hers was not a standard Starfleet-issue chair. It was a sort of throne, high-backed but with thick, colorful cushions that undercut its formality.

"Well, I certainly hope you don't mind if *I* sit." And she did so with a flourish and a hint of a grin.

"I don't have time for this," snapped Janeway, stepping forward. Her hands went to her hips. "Are you a member of the Q Continuum? You're certainly behaving like one."

Tialin's brown eyes brightened. "Ah, the Q. Most amusing. Tricky folk, though, don't you find?"

"No trickier than you," said Telek, unable to contain himself further. He stepped forward. "We are dying. My people back in the Alpha Quadrant are dying, and all because of Shepherd intervention! You said we were right to be suspicious if we had encountered Lhiau. Is he one of you?"

"Yes and no," Tialin replied. "As I said, it's a long story. Suffice it to say that Lhiau *was* one of us, before he turned renegade." Her flip tone vanished and she sat up straight in the chair. "We do not condone what he has done and is trying to do, for a variety of reasons, some of which you know. We do not tinker with life. Lhiau and a few others are rogues—wild, unpredictable, and utterly untrustworthy. We deeply regret what he has done to you and will certainly give you all the aid we can."

Suddenly, Chakotay felt the hard knot of annoyance that had rested icily in his gut dissolve. Janeway's face, seemingly permanently furrowed, relaxed. One hand went to her temple.

"It's gone," she said softly. "The headache."

Out of the corner of his eye, Chakotay saw the Doctor glance at his tricorder. He expected to see him smile, to announce that the readings were back to normal. Instead, the hologram frowned but remained silent.

Tialin smiled benevolently and inclined her head like a goddess graciously accepting worship. She extended a hand, and a sphere manifested in her palm. It was similar to the one from which she had appeared, but smaller and less intensely colorful.

"Gaze into the sphere," she said, sounding like a Gypsy fortune-teller of old. "See there, caught safely, the First Things which have so plagued you. We have removed every trace of altered dark matter from your bodies and your vessels, and have contained it all within this sphere. I have rendered it visible to your limited range of viewing. It will trouble you and your crew no longer."

Chakotay found himself responding to the singsong voice, and he peered at the orb as he had been instructed. At first he could see nothing, and he wondered if this was some kind of Shepherd joke. But then, fleetingly, he saw something glitter and then disappear. He blinked.

"I saw something," he said to Janeway, who met his gaze and nodded.

"I did too. Thank you, Tialin."

"So tiny to be such a danger, is it not?" mused Tialin, looking intently at the sphere. Her expression turned mischievous. She turned suddenly and tossed the orb to Paris. "Catch!"

Chakotay felt his heart stop for a second as the sphere flew through the air. Reflexively, Tom caught it in his good hand and Chakotay began to breathe again.

"Tialin, we have so many questions," said Chakotay. "I wouldn't even know where to begin."

"You want to know what dark matter is," said Tialin firmly. "I will tell you a little about it. Dark matter particles were the First Things to fill the universes. They exist simultaneously in all universes, but completely in none of them. It is this quality that makes the First Things so elusive, so hard for beings such as yourselves to understand with your limited cognitive capacities."

Janeway ignored the slur, her eyes bright with interest, and nodded her comprehension. "That's why we can measure it. It's got gravity; we can calculate the gravitational pull, but we can't see it or touch it in any way. Unless it comes into contact with subspace, which renders it—"

Her eyes widened. "So that's what Lhiau is doing. He's pulling the dark matter completely into this universe by using Telek's wormholes!"

Tialin nodded. "For a lower species—no offense, Captain—you grasp theoretical truths quite quickly. Good. I am glad fate has brought us together. Yes, Lhiau is bringing dark matter fully into your universe. He is rendering it solid, visible, and extremely deadly by doing so."

"Of course," said the Doctor. "That's why Seven was able to see the dark-matter shielding. Her ocular implant is able to detect irregularities or disruptions in space-time. If the dark matter doesn't exist fully in one universe, that certainly qualifies as a disruption in space-time. A naturally occurring one, but a disruption nonetheless."

"Lhiau is tampering with something he should not." Tialin's shrewd gaze flickered from one face to another. "You must help us stop him."

"How?" Telek was angry and puzzled. "How are we to stop Lhiau? We cannot even fully comprehend why he is doing what he is doing and how!"

"As I said, you needed our help. We have helped you by extracting and containing all the dark matter in your bodies and equipment. Now, you must help others. We gift this technology to you. Lhiau's tampering has far-reaching consequences. The mutated dark matter he has released has spread in all directions. Some lies ahead of you, attacking new systems you have never encountered; some lies behind you, destroying places you have already been. And some are even manifesting . . . elsewhere."

Chakotay thought of the dozens of wormholes, each one spewing deadly amounts of dark matter into the surrounding space. Neutrinos, they knew, traveled at the speed of light. How fast was dark matter? How many systems had Lhiau's dark matter affected by now?

Tialin's lips curved in a smile. "Your ship is called *Voyager,* Captain Janeway. You have already proved it an aptly named vessel. Now, you must temporarily halt your journey to the Alpha Quadrant for an even better cause—saving countless beings from the fate that you have so narrowly escaped yourselves. I am sending you on a quest—a crusade, if you like."

Tialin leaned forward, her eyes wide and unblinking. "We will give you the ability to locate and contain the mutated dark matter. Your task is to take the sphere and travel everywhere you can, gathering it up, piece by dangerous piece."

"Wait a minute," interrupted Paris, sounding much more like himself than he had for the last several days. "You're sending us to do your job for you? You seem pretty darn near omnipotent to me. Can't you just wave your hands and make all this right again?"

Tialin rose and went to him, staring him down. "Our job is to halt Lhiau and his rogues before they do still more harm. And to answer your question, no. We are *not* omnipotent tricksters like the Q. For which you should be grateful, because if we were, Lhiau would have done far worse damage than setting loose mutated dark matter particles upon an unsuspecting universe!"

Paris backed up a step before the frail-seeming being. Tialin continued. "Far, far more is at stake than I am permitted to tell you, yet I would have thought that saving innocent lives would have been sufficient motivation and explanation. Perhaps you are not as evolved as you think!"

"But . . . you will take care of Lhiau?" persisted Telek. "You will save my people? They do not know what they are doing, what kind of monster they have allied with."

Gently, Tialin laid a wizened hand on the Romulan's uniformed shoulder. "We know of your pain, and we are doing everything we can. Which," she added, throwing Paris a glance, "is not inconsiderable, despite our limitations. Captain, the decision is yours. You will not be punished by us in any way if you decide not to accept this quest. But know that you will be doing a great deal of good, more," she added, emphasizing the words, "than you yet know."

Chakotay knew his captain. He didn't for a minute think she would decide other than what she stated firmly: "We accept." How could they not? After seeing the dreadful things this mutated dark matter wrought upon the innocent, how could they not do everything they could to prevent that kind of atrocity from happening to someone else?

At that precise moment, the cavern was flooded with a blinding light. Someone screamed. It was the woman they had found, Khala.

"No!" she was crying. "No, not again, not to another dead place—"

Chakotay shielded his face from the light, her words chilling his soul. This was the same brilliant illumination they had witnessed from the safety of their bridge a few hours earlier, the same light that had heralded the transformation of a vibrant class-M planet into a dying, churning rock in the span of a few heartbeats. Khala had claimed that she had been brought here at the same time that the planet had blinked out of and then into existence again.

He opened his eyes a slit and through the veil of lashes was just barely able to make out that something was happening. The light was emanating from a single point, to the right and up, close to the stone ceiling of the cavern. Out of nowhere tumbled two large rocks and a huge shower of dust. Paris was right in their path.

Reacting without even thinking, Chakotay dove for the younger man, knocking him out of harm's way with the force of his own body. As Paris hit the earth, crying out with the pain the impact caused his broken arm, the orb Tialin had tossed to him fell out of his hand. It landed hard on the stone but did not break. It bounced twice, then rolled to a stop, its dreadful contents still safely imprisoned. Dust and debris showered Chakotay and Paris, but the stones did not strike them.

All of this happened in the fraction of a second. Coughing, Chakotay turned his head to look at the bright opening from which the rocks had tumbled.

And suddenly, Chakotay understood. Everything. Khala, the dead planet, the Shepherds, the true nature of dark matter—he comprehended it all and knew what he had to do.

There was no time to even warn Janeway, no opportunity to impart this sudden blinding knowledge to his captain. Already, the light around the aperture was dimming, and soon the precious opportunity would be missed. Chakotay hauled Paris to his feet and ran, dragging the ensign with him, toward the light.

He leaped through.

The portal vanished.

"Chakotay!" cried Janeway. The cavern now

seemed dark to her after the brightness of the portal. She ran to the rocks, touched them, trying to find a lingering trace of the opening into which her first officer and friend had leaped.

There was nothing, no trace. "That's exactly what happened the first time!" said Khala, trembling. "I was pulled through, I hit the ground, and then . . . then it vanished."

Janeway whirled on Tialin. "What have you done with Chakotay and Paris?" she demanded.

Tialin looked regretful. *"I* have done nothing with them. But do not fear, Captain Janeway."

But Janeway wasn't having any of it. "Your rogues toy with our lives, infect us, you call us here, you obliterate life on an entire planet—"

"I told you, Captain, and I dislike repeating myself," said Tialin, a touch of irritation in her voice. "No one forced Commander Chakotay to leap through the portal. Perhaps he is the wisest of you, after all. He understood—I should say, understands."

"But this planet, Khala—what the hell is going on? Where are my crewmen?"

Her combadge chirped. "Kim to Janeway."

Startled, Janeway replied, "Janeway here. Go ahead, Ensign. I want to hear some good news."

"Well," and Kim's voice was higher than usual, "I've got bad news first. It's the Romulans. They've found us."

CHAPTER

15

"STATUS REPORT," SNAPPED JANEWAY.

"There are thirteen warbirds, all cloaked," said Kim. "They're still on long-distance scanners but they're closing in fast. We're able to detect them only because Telek has informed us how to locate the dark-matter cloaking. Shields are up, and we've gone to Red Alert."

"How's *Voyager?*" the captain asked.

"I'm guessing you found the Shepherds," said Kim, "because everything on the ship has been fixed. It's in perfect operating order. Not a trace of dark matter on board, and everyone who's been affected by it is back to normal."

"Even Neelix?"

"Even Neelix." Harry's voice was warm, even in this moment of crisis. "He wanted me to tell Telek

R'Mor he planned to cook him a banquet by way of apology."

Janeway looked at Tialin, who put a hand to her heart and bowed in acknowledgment.

"You're right. We found the Shepherds, Harry. And it sounds like it wasn't a minute too soon, either. Keep those shields up. We can't take the risk of lowering them for you to beam us up. Besides, we're trapped deep inside a mountain, and I doubt the transporter could even lock on to us here."

She was angry, frustrated, and heartsick. Chakotay and Tom had vanished to who knew where. She wondered if they were even still alive. Their ship was now clean of the mutated dark matter, but thirteen—*thirteen!*—Romulan warbirds were descending on them even as she spoke with Harry. Those weren't odds she liked. And here she was, stuck inside this mountain while *Voyager* was about to plunge into a dreadful battle with young Harry Kim in the captain's chair.

Do not fear, child.

The voice was inside Janeway's head, and calm spread over her like a blanket at the words. It was Tialin, of course. But Janeway felt comforted by the telepathic contact in a way that her verbal exchange with Tialin had not permitted. It was a maternal embrace of the mind and spirit, and Janeway knew all at once that yes, despite her mysteries and playful superiority, Tialin could be trusted.

Your friends are safe and where they need to be. And I would not think of depriving you of the excitement of such a battle.

All at once, Janeway found herself on the bridge. Telek R'Mor, startled, stood at her right side and looked about. The Doctor and Khala were not present; Janeway imagined they were in sickbay.

"Torres to bridge. What the hell is this floating ball that just materialized in engineering?"

"Janeway here," the captain replied. "I'll explain it all once we're out of danger, Lieutenant. In the meantime, just keep an eye on it."

"It is good to see you, Captain," came Tuvok's smooth, ice-cream-cool voice. Janeway glanced over her shoulder, and pleasure filled her as she saw her old friend standing erect at his post. It was wonderful to see him well again.

"And you, Tuvok."

"Commander Chakotay and Ensign Paris?"

"Later. I think they're all right, though."

"Captain." Kim's voice was taut. "They're within viewing range."

"Flee them, Captain," said Telek. "Your ship has the superior speed."

Janeway considered the option, then shook her head. "No. I owe it to them to at least try to reason with them, warn them about what's going on."

"They will not listen!" Telek cried. "Do you not think that if I believed for a moment they would, I would suggest flight? These centurions are under the direct command of the Tal Shiar, Captain. They have not come to talk, they have come to conquer, and if they cannot conquer, then they will die. That is and has always been our way."

His angry words confirmed Janeway's fears, but she stuck by her decision. "I still have to try. Besides, you heard Tialin. Our job is to gather the dark matter that's been scattered throughout the quadrant. If we run away now, the Romulans will pursue us to the best of their ability, distributing still more dark matter among innocent star systems. No, Telek. I can't permit that to happen."

Her blue eyes gleamed. "We make our stand here. We reason, or we fight. Two options. And if we fight, we live or we die." She turned to Telek and regarded him steadily. "Two options."

"If I may, then," said Telek with admirable calm, "I should like to remain on the bridge. They may listen to one of their own."

"Dr. R'Mor," said Tuvok. "You are a traitor as far as the Romulans are concerned. I do not think they will be inclined to pay any heed to anything you say. Your presence on this bridge might be a detriment if we do manage to open negotiations."

"You still think me untrustworthy, is that it, Tuvok?" asked R'Mor sadly.

"No," said Tuvok, surprising Janeway. "I trust you completely. It is your comrades in the Alpha Quadrant whom I do not trust."

"Stay, Telek," said Janeway. "You have the right to be a witness, if nothing else." As she gazed at the screen, which still showed nothing but stars and black space, she saw Chakotay's empty chair out of the corner of her eye and felt a sudden ache.

Chakotay. Please be all right, wherever you are.

Ensign Jenkins had taken Paris's place at the conn, her fair hair a touch longer than Paris's, and Janeway silently mourned Tom's absence as well.

"They're within visual range."

Janeway didn't ask for it to be put on screen. There would be nothing to see. She instead touched a lighted button at her side, and her personal viewscreen moved slowly into place. On the computer screen, she could see the Romulan ships as she could not with her own eyes: thirteen of them, their graphic symbols etched pale green, advancing with a single purpose upon her ship.

"Mr. Kim, open a hailing frequency."

"Channel's open, Captain."

Her eyes on the tiny symbolic ships, Janeway said, "This is Captain Kathryn Janeway of the Federation *Starship Voyager.* We have the ability to detect your dark-matter cloak and compensate accordingly. We must warn you that the dark matter is affecting your vessels and your bodies. It is dangerous and will eventually destroy you. We have the technology to remove all dark matter from your ships. We have done so with our own vessel. Please, call off this attack and let us discuss how to help you."

Silence. "No response, Captain. They didn't even open a channel to receive it."

"As I said," said Telek heavily. "They will not listen."

Still, Janeway tried again. "Our two governments are not at war. You are in grave danger. I repeat, halt your attack and we will give you the information to prove that we are telling you the truth."

Still nothing. Harry Kim shook his head.

Briefly, Janeway closed her eyes. Like everyone else in Starfleet, she'd been taught a suspicious dislike of the mysterious, exotic, dangerous Romulans. Telek R'Mor's first visit had done much to dissipate that old prejudice, and the extended time she had shared with him on this second encounter had shattered it utterly.

Oh, certainly she had problems with their government's policies. And it appeared that even the Romulans themselves had disagreements with the shadowy Tal Shiar. But at the end of the day, the Romulans were people, individuals, even the members of the Tal Shiar and the senators. They had wives, husbands, children, parents; they laughed and wept and enjoyed good food and drink and art just like anybody else.

Those centurions aboard the vessels had, by stubbornly refusing to listen to what *Voyager* had to say, figuratively signed their death warrants. If they were not destroyed outright in the battle that was about to begin at any moment, they would die soon nonetheless, and die horribly, from the ravages of the mutated dark matter upon their bodies.

Damn it all to hell.

"They're powering up their weapons, Captain," said Kim.

And so it began.

Jekri Kaleh frowned at the poor transmission she was receiving from the lead vessel. They had barely been able to receive the signal from one of the scout-ships a few days ago. It had been spotty and erratic, and more than once Jekri had wrestled with the icy certainty that they were being led down a frag-mented, inaccurate path. She had claimed several precious hours double-checking the coordinates, making sure that the thirteen cloaked warbirds would manifest near *Voyager* and not near the greedy maw of an unexpected black hole or, just as bad from her point of view, nowhere near the Feder-ation starship that was their quarry.

Finally, all was in readiness. Jekri had taken a deep breath and given the order that sent thirteen warbirds, cloaked in undetectable dark matter, through the wormhole that Telek R'Mor's encrypted notes had enabled them to create.

Her heart thudded rapidly in her abdomen, and she felt sweat break beneath her arms and on her sculpted forehead. Jekri had longed to lead the ves-sels in this, their moment of ultimate triumph, but such an honor had been granted to thirteen members of the Senate, all of whom, she had no doubt, were owed favors by the Praetor, the Proconsul, or the Empress herself. Each stood on the bridge of a war-bird, an honorary general in this sweetest of battles. She, chairman of the Tal Shiar, the mastermind of the whole project, would linger behind, observing the fight as it transpired, dwelling in the shadows of power as she had always done.

She had not even been permitted to speak to the captains and their crews before the warbirds embarked. That had rankled, and still irked her. But she would know, when they returned from the Delta Quadrant with a glorious spoil of war in tow, who was responsible.

"Why, yes," came an unctuous voice at her ear. "Thank you. It *is* entirely due to me. How kind of you to acknowledge it."

Jekri's face did not move a muscle, but she could not control the rush of hot green blood to her soft cheeks. It was as she had suspected: Lhiau had greater powers than he was revealing. For the first time in her life, she wished she were a Vulcan. They at least knew forms of mental control that inhibited telepathic eavesdropping, something she regarded as the lowest form of cowardice imaginable.

Lhiau grunted at her angry thoughts and turned his attention to the viewscreen. At the console, Verrak sat stiff and angry. Jekri couldn't read minds, but it was ease itself to read Verrak's body language after so many years spent serving with him. He was excited about the upcoming battle, worried about its outcome, and disgusted with Lhiau.

All emotions she shared completely. She and he were so alike, sometimes, though she sometimes grew cold in reaction to something at which he grew hot. Still, he had proved himself time and again a good and loyal comrade.

"Have you been able to clarify the signal at all?" she asked.

"Negative, Chairman. This is the best I have been able to do."

"The damn wormhole," sighed Lhiau. "Your Telek R'Mor may be the finest scientist Romulus has produced, but that really isn't saying much, is it?"

"Again, I invite you to lend your clearly superior knowledge to this endeavor," said Jekri through clenched teeth, aware of the sarcasm but unable to stop it bleeding into her words. "You came to us, you demanded we find Dr. R'Mor—"

"And I have given you the precious dark matter which is, if you are intelligent enough to use it properly, the key to your conquest of the universe!"

"Why do I think that our conquest of the universe has nothing to do with the reason you're here?" At last she voiced the question she had been longing to ask. "Why *are* you here, Lhiau? What is it you want from us? How high is the price?"

Jekri felt a sudden, stabbing pain in her temples and couldn't suppress a faint gasp of agony. All at once, it was gone. Lhiau, of course. Despite the pain she'd just endured, she was pleased. She was, finally, starting to get under his skin.

I do not like you. I do not trust you. I will obey my superiors, but the moment we have done with you I will come for you. She thought the thought as clearly and precisely as possible.

Foolish Little Dagger. You tell me nothing I do not already know, and certainly nothing I fear.

Let him rot, then. She returned her attention to the viewscreen, frowning again at the lack of clarity of the transmission. Perhaps R'Mor was correct and the wormhole was interfering.

"They've cleared the wormhole," said Verrak, and his voice was tense. Jekri couldn't help herself. A slow smile tugged at her lips, and she placed a hand on Verrak's shoulder and squeezed briefly.

Her pleasure was short-lived. "Dammit, the transmission is just as bad as before. Why didn't it clear up once they left the wormhole?"

"Something inside Telek's wormhole may have damaged the ships," said Lhiau. "It wouldn't surprise me at all."

She ignored him. Despite the fuzzy, erratic picture, it was sufficiently clear for her to make out the shape of the Federation vessel. *Voyager.* She would belong to Jekri soon.

The ships fanned out into attack pattern gamma, surrounding the ship and approaching at angles that ensured that they could fire on the ship without harming another vessel on the opposite side.

"Target weapons and propulsion," she said aloud, as if she were the one on the bridge of the lead ship. "Do not damage the ship if you can help it. We want this lamb whole and only hamstrung, not bleeding to death."

"Target their weapons and propulsion systems," said Janeway. There was no point in firing a warning shot across the bow of one of the vessels. The Romulans had already been warned, and it had clearly made no difference.

Out of the seeming emptiness of space there appeared the glow of a photon torpedo. "Evasive maneuvers!" cried Janeway, and Jenkins obediently dove.

"Firing again," said Kim. The attack had come from another one of the thirteen vessels, and this time there was no chance to avoid it. The ship shuddered a little under the direct hit.

"Shields are holding," intoned Tuvok. "Down six percent."

"Only six?" Janeway was amazed. The attack had been on target and severe. The damage ought to have been much, much worse.

"The dark matter has apparently begun damaging the effectiveness of the Romulans' weapons systems." Tuvok glanced up. "However, the attack has also scattered mutated dark matter throughout our shields. Damage is already beginning."

"Are you saying it's more virulent than before?"

"Firing again," interrupted Kim.

Janeway cursed softly and gripped her chair. Another direct hit, and it felt harder this time. "Return fire," she ordered Tuvok.

The ship swung around, and on her screen Janeway saw that they had locked on to one of the ships, although the main viewscreen showed nothing at all.

Tuvok fired.

The ship exploded.

So did the ship immediately beside it.

Janeway shielded her eyes from the dreadful brightness. "What just happened?" she demanded.

"I don't know," said Kim, his fingers flying. "It just . . . blew up."

"We targeted their weapons systems, per your orders, Captain," said Tuvok. "The attack should not have destroyed the warbird."

Another ship fired again. Again, *Voyager* trembled. "Shields down twenty-two percent," Tuvok said. "They are permeated with dark matter."

"Janeway to engineering. Torres, has there been any reaction by that glowing sphere to the battle?"

"Negative, Captain. Should there have been?"

"I'm not sure." *Dammit. Tialin, you're sure as hell not making this easy for us. I thought that thing you gave us caught dark matter and ate it for breakfast.* "Status report?"

"For a while there, we seemed to have gotten rid of all the dark matter on the ship. Now it's back."

"It's the Romulan ships," said Telek. "They are saturated with dark matter particles. Do you remember the centurions and their scoutship? It has taken longer because there are more people and more systems to infect, but that is surely what is occurring on all thirteen of those vessels." He corrected himself. "Eleven vessels, now."

He looked heartsick. "Every time they activate their cloak, every moment that they have it operating, they are increasing their dosage of dark matter exponentially. And that is what we are being bombarded with."

Janeway nodded her comprehension and relayed the new information to B'Elanna. "Every time we're fired upon, they hit us not only with their weapons, but with a dose of mutated dark matter that's apparently only gotten more dangerous with time. Do what you can, Torres. Janeway out."

She sank back in her chair. Again a Romulan fired, and this time the ship rocked violently. "Shields down thirty-one percent," said Kim. "Casualties reported on decks thirteen, twelve, and eight."

Janeway made a decision. She ached with the choice, but sometimes being a captain of a starship meant that you had to make the tough decisions. She could not put her crew at risk any longer. The Romulans had had their chances—plenty of them. She sensed rather than saw Telek R'Mor straighten behind her, as if he could read her mind and knew what she had decided.

"Target another vessel. Aim for their weapons or propulsion." Not that it would make any difference, but it might help her sleep better.

She swallowed, knowing what would happen, then gave the order. "Fire."

Red phaser energy screamed across space. The Romulan ship exploded on impact, pieces of invisible metal hurtling outward. The fire was visible, however, a rolling orange, red, and white ball of destruction before space inevitably consumed it.

"No life-signs, Captain," said Kim quietly.

"Open a channel, Mr. Kim. Hell, open them all. Broadcast on every frequency the following message from now until . . . until this is over, one way or another."

"Go ahead," said Kim.

"Captain Janeway to Romulan vessels: We have no

wish to destroy your ships or injure your crew, but we will defend ourselves as long as we are attacked. Your ships are vulnerable because of their dark-matter cloaks. Please, I beg you, call off this attack and let us give you the information to save yourselves!"

"Message being broadcast, Captain." Kim hesitated, then, "No response or acknowledgment."

Telek R'Mor had been right. They would conquer, or they would die.

"The ships are too fragile," said the Romulan scientist softly. "Their own shields have done this to them. One volley and they are done for. Our magnificent warbirds . . ." His voice trailed off.

Janeway glanced down at her viewscreen. There were ten of the ships now. Even as she counted, two torpedoes, fired in rapid succession, rocked the ship violently. She heard the sizzle that marked fire on the bridge and a muffled cry from young Garan, who was manning the science station. An acrid stench stung her nose, and almost immediately she felt pain in her leg. She'd strained a tendon trying to keep her seat. Her injured wrists ached in harmonious sympathy but, deliberately, Janeway forced the cry of her wounded body out of her mind.

"Fire at will, Tuvok. Kim, keep broadcasting that message. I want to know the minute someone tries to respond. Is that understood?"

"Aye, Captain," Kim replied, but he didn't look hopeful. There was a nasty cut on his forehead and he wiped absently at the trickle of red before it got into his eye.

The next few minutes passed like a hallucination for *Voyager*'s captain. The ship swung about, locating Romulan vessels despite the cloaks that would be their deaths, locking on, firing. Shot after shot, blast after blast, in a peculiarly dreamy dance of destruction. It didn't seem so bad when you couldn't see the ships blowing up in front of your eyes, when you could only see the fireballs. And yet, people were dying.

Harry Kim said nothing.

Down to seven warbirds, now. There would be those hawks in the Federation who would find pleasure in the fact that a single Starfleet vessel had held its own against thirteen ships, had indeed destroyed six of them outright. Janeway was not among them.

Despite the automatic fire extinguishers, the bridge was beginning to smell of smoke. It stung Janeway's blue eyes and she blinked back the tears. Beside her, Telek R'Mor had sunk into Chakotay's chair. He leaned forward, his hands clasped between his knees, his eyes fixed on the viewscreen and the ships he could not see as they attacked, only as they were destroyed.

Another direct hit on one ship, with two explosions. The ship next to the first one had been destroyed as a result of the dreadful dark matter that had burst upon it like spores from a deadly plant.

Five left now.

"For the love of God," whispered Janeway, "contact us, damn you!"

"What is happening?" The question was a scream, ripped from Jekri's throat as she watched the ships being destroyed one by one, sometimes two by two.

"I would think that was obvious," said Lhiau. "Your mighty warbirds are getting the *llhrei* beaten out of them."

"This is not possible," Jekri breathed, her hands clenching into impotent fists. "We were thirteen. They couldn't see us coming. Even if they knew we were tracking them, they *shouldn't* have been able to target us like that!"

"The traitor Telek," said Lhiau. "He has told them how to find your ships."

"Even R'Mor could not penetrate the dark-matter shielding," said Verrak sharply. He still clung to his idea that Telek had been abducted, had not been a traitor. Sometimes Verrak had oddly romantic—and dangerous—notions. Jekri would have upbraided him had they been alone, but did not want Lhiau to see any division in their ranks.

"He could have learned. He knows more than any of you pathetic—" With a disgusted growl, Lhiau didn't even bother to complete his sentence.

Jekri stared at the grainy image. There was no sound. Before her eyes, yet another fireball roiled up and then dissipated.

"How many left?" she asked Verrak.

He glanced up at her, pain in his handsome face. "Five," he said bluntly. "The Federations have been hailing the ships. We have not listened to their message. Perhaps we should."

"Negative. They would say anything to save their ship."

"Most honored Chairman," Verrak said, "they do not have to do anything to save their ship. They are *winning.*"

Even as he spoke, Jekri watched another warbird, a ship they had thought invincible, explode into invisible debris. Hundreds were aboard each ship.

She made her decision, though it killed something inside her to do it. Jekri leaned forward, thumbing a control on the console so hard it hurt her hand.

"Chairman Kaleh to lead vessel. Retreat. Repeat, retreat at once. There are to be no more lives wasted this day."

"But we must get Telek, we must—" Lhiau began.

"You are to be silent!" All traces of composure that Jekri might have had had evaporated with her last order. Tears of bitterness and rage spilled from her gray eyes, and she was not ashamed of them. She advanced on Lhiau like a *hnoiyika* closing in for the kill, and even though she knew his powers probably rendered him able to slay her with a thought, she saw him take a step backward.

"Thousands—thousands, do you understand?—of brave Romulans have died in this battle today, and I will not tolerate your sneers and belittlement of their sacrifice. Silence, Lhiau, silence, and if you cannot be silent of your own choice than I shall make you be silent!"

Their gazes locked, and it was Lhiau who looked away first.

* * *

"They're retreating, Captain," Kim announced. Janeway could see it on her screen. "Should we pursue?"

"Negative, Ensign. Let them go."

Kim glanced uneasily at Tuvok, then back at his captain. "They've seen us fight," he said. "They have a better grasp now of what *Voyager* is capable of. If they take that first-hand knowledge back to the Alpha Quadrant, we risk polluting the timeline."

Still Janeway shook her head. "It's already been polluted. They lost hundreds here, Mr. Kim. They sent all thirteen ships equipped with dark-matter cloaks against us, and only five are limping home. They can't hurt us any more. I won't follow them and hunt them down to the last man. Besides, that might cause more damage to the timeline than we've already done. Who knows what contributions someone aboard one of those ships might make one day. We could be killing the Romulan who later guides his people to an alliance with the Federation."

"You are merciful, Captain Janeway," said Telek.

Janeway stared at the screen, momentarily lost in the image of bright white stars and black space. "I don't know that the Romulans aboard those eight ships would share your opinion, Dr. R'Mor."

"The five ships have entered the wormhole," said Kim.

"Safe journey home," whispered Janeway, softly. "Cancel Red—"

"Captain!" said Kim. "The five ships—there

231

seems to be some kind of problem with two of them. They're disintegrating."

"Oh, no," breathed Janeway. She rose from her chair, wincing with pain, and made her way over to Ops. "Monitor them." The dark matter. The damned, damned dark matter.

"The first vessel has made it safely out of the wormhole. So has the second. There goes the third . . . ."

But it never materialized on the other side. As Janeway watched, eyes glued to the screen, the three ships still in the wormhole disappeared. There was a flash on the viewscreen. The wormhole had collapsed, probably because one of the vessels had exploded inside it. Of the thirteen mighty warbirds that had ventured through the wormhole, intent on capturing a glorious prize and returning home victors, only two had survived.

"We've lost contact," said Kim, unnecessarily. His voice was somber.

Janeway glanced up to find Telek R'Mor gazing at her. "I'm so sorry," she said.

"Sorrow will not bring back the dead," he said, his voice harsh with pain.

"Engineering to Janeway. Captain, you've got to tell me about this sphere, I can't make heads or—"

"Sickbay to Captain Janeway. I've learned a few interesting things about our guest that I think—"

"One at a time!" exclaimed Janeway. "Doctor, is this a medical emergency?"

"No," replied the Doctor, somewhat huffily, "but nonetheless I think—"

"Then we're off to engineering. I want that dark matter off my ship and I want it off now. Tuvok, you have the bridge. Doctor R'Mor, please come with me. We'll need your knowledge as well."

As they headed for the turbolift, Janeway thought to herself that the Shepherds might have raised more questions than they answered.

CHAPTER
16

B'ELANNA LOOKED HER USUAL CAPABLE SELF AS SHE glanced up when her captain and Tuvok entered. "What is this thing?" she asked without preamble, gesticulating with the hand that held the Shepherd's sphere.

"How's the stomach?" Janeway asked first, smiling a little.

Torres grimaced. "Fine, now, thank goodness."

Janeway's smile faded. "Lieutenant, I have some bad news. It's about Tom."

B'Elanna's face went very still. She stood up a bit straighter, bracing herself. "What happened?"

"Both he and Chakotay have disappeared. It's a long story, about what happened when we encountered the Shepherd, and you'll be fully briefed later, but essentially they went through some kind of portal. The Shepherd, Tialin, assured me that they were both where they needed to be, that they would be all right. And although there wasn't time to confirm anything, Chakotay seemed to know exactly what he was doing. It was obvious he chose to go through the portal, and to take Tom with him."

Torres swallowed, but her composure was admirable. "Will . . . will we see them again?"

"I certainly hope so, B'Elanna," said Janeway fervently. "There's reason to believe that regardless of whether they return, they'll be all right."

She realized her reassurance was almost fulsome, as if she were creating a reality with her words. Torres didn't miss it, either, and when she unexpectedly reached out to squeeze her captain's shoulder, Janeway didn't mind. They had both lost people they cared deeply about and, in a sense, were sisters in that loss.

"I understand, Captain. Now," and Torres squared her shoulders, "about this ball?"

"This ball," said Janeway, "holds every bit of the dark matter that was aboard this ship."

Torres looked at the sphere with a new respect. "Tialin somehow managed to trap all the mutated dark matter in there and render it harmless," Janeway continued. "Look at it closely. She even made it visible to us."

Torres peered into the orb. "Yes, I can just see them, if I don't look directly at it—tiny little things. So this is what caused all that damage? Right in here?"

Janeway nodded. "It seems amazing, doesn't it?"

"Tialin also said that we would be given the technology with which to trap other particles of mutated dark matter," said Telek. "But this orb did not seem to function properly while we were under attack. We were again bombarded with particles of dark matter from the Romulan ships, and again it damaged *Voyager.* Tialin would seem to be lying to us."

Gently, Janeway took the small orb from Torres and tossed it up and down, much like a child's toy. She knew, as Torres could not, that the sphere was unbreakable.

"Perhaps not, Telek. Tialin said she would give us the technology, and I've got it right here in my hand. But it seems as though she left it up to us to figure out how to make this technology work." She raised an eyebrow. "How did she know we enjoy challenges so much?"

She returned the ball to Torres. "Get Seven in here. You'll be working with Dr. R'Mor on figuring out what makes this little ball tick. I'm sure the three of you will come up with something."

For a moment, the situation struck her as powerfully significant. The three of them. They were a half-Klingon former rebel, a Borg freed from the collective, and a high-ranking Romulan scientist. Together they would combine their skills and determine a way to extract deadly matter, information which, according to Tialin, could save untold lives.

Torres looked at her expectantly, unable to decipher her expression. Janeway smiled reassuringly.

"Carry on," she said.

The door hissed open, and the Doctor looked up from examining their visitor. "Captain Janeway. How good of you to grace us with your presence."

Still giddy with the image of union among enemies she'd just experienced in engineering, Janeway let the Doctor's gibe pass unchallenged. She glanced briefly at Shamraa Khala Remilkansuur, who was seated on one of the beds, but then gave her full attention to her own crew member.

"Neelix," she said, saying volumes with the single word. She reached out her hands to him, and he clasped them tightly. "What are you still doing here? Harry said you were fine."

"Last time I checked, Ensign Kim had not gotten a medical degree," said the Doctor. "Although now that you mention his name, right now I do need an extra pair of hands. Since Mr. Paris is . . . unavailable, I'll make do with what I've got. Sickbay to Ensign Kim."

"Kim here."

"Are you able to report to sickbay and assist me?"

A pause, presumably while Kim checked with Tuvok, then, "Certainly. On my way."

"I'm keeping Mr. Neelix here for another few hours while I run some tests and observe his behavior," said the Doctor. "It wouldn't do to unleash him on an unsuspecting mess hall without making certain he's completely recovered. He does quite enough damage with his cooking when he's well." But the

Doctor softened the words with a smile, an almost unconscious one. Janeway liked it.

Neelix had picked up on the Doctor's comment and asked, "What happened to Tom? Is he all right?"

Janeway closed her eyes, then opened them again. Briefly, she told Neelix about Tom and Chakotay. She was beginning to hate going through this again and again. She needed to make a shipwide announcement soon, once she'd put out all these last little fires.

Neelix looked crushed. "Oh," was all he said in a small, soft voice.

"I really believe they'll be all right," she said, echoing the words she'd said to Torres. "Now. How are *you* doing?"

"I'm feeling fine, Captain," Neelix assured her, still clasping her hands as he sat on the bed. "But I'm all for following the Doctor's orders." His face fell. "They tell me that I attacked Dr. R'Mor. I have no memory of such a dreadful thing. I can't believe it."

"We couldn't either," his captain assured him. "That's the first clue we had that there was something very wrong. No one blames you, Neelix. You were infected with the dark matter."

His whiskers drooped. "Still, I feel just terrible about it. I'll work extra shifts, I'll donate my replicator rations, anything to make it up to that poor man."

Janeway squeezed Neelix's hands, then let them go. "I'm sure that of all of us, Dr. R'Mor best appreciates how dark matter affects people. There's no grudge, Neelix. Though," she added, "if you want to brew up a pot of that new coffee substitute you've been working on, I think we could all use some."

"Coming right up!" The Talaxian started to slip off the bed. The Doctor cleared his throat. Neelix, chastened, climbed back up. "Once the Doctor has released me, of course." Sighing, he lay back down on the bed, twiddling his thumbs impatiently.

Janeway looked around, the smile on her lips fading. Carefully surrounded by stasis fields were the bodies of the two Romulan centurions and that of Ensign Kirby. Johnson had apparently made it, but the bombardment of dark matter had been too much for Kirby. Once there was a moment to slow down, to think, to breathe again, the three would be placed into the smooth, round-edged Starfleet coffins and sent off into space with all honors, the Romulan soldiers as well as her own loyal crewman.

She hated this. Hated loss of life. Gamely, Janeway squared her shoulders, grateful that the next leg of the journey provided opportunities to save lives, not take them. She turned to the visitor aboard her ship.

"How are you feeling, Khala?" she asked.

"Fine, thank you, Captain," the woman replied. "Although, according to your Doctor, I shouldn't be."

The Doctor was fairly quivering with information he wished to deliver. Janeway turned to him. "Out with it, Doctor. What's going on?"

"I truly wish I knew," he replied, startling her. "Come here and let me show you something." She followed him to his office, where he impatiently punched up some schematics.

"You will recall my exasperation with the tricorder when we first attempted to scan Khala," said the Doctor. "I had thought that the dark matter was distorting my readings, but apparently, they were accurate."

The information the Doctor showed her was no different from the confused jumble he'd had her look at earlier. The scientist in her was excited by the bizarre readings, but in her position as captain, she knew they represented yet another puzzle they'd have to unravel.

The DNA sequence was indeed backward. The whole thing looked like some young Academy student's idea of a joke. According to the laws of science and physics as she understood them, Khala ought not to exist.

Yet there she was, a beautiful young woman painted in shades of blue, looking around curiously at their sickbay. Janeway regarded her for a moment: a lost, frightened soul, no doubt as confused as they as to why she was here.

The door hissed open and Ensign Kim entered. "Good," said the Doctor. "You can help me run another series of tests on Khala."

Kim did a double take at the attractive alien female in sickbay. "Hello," he said, a little shyly. She smiled at him in return. Kim turned to Janeway. Privately, he said, "Captain, what's going on? Where are Tom and Chakotay? And who is—"

"I'm going to make a shipwide announcement shortly, Harry." She squeezed his shoulder. "But I think everything's going to be all right." Quickly

Janeway downloaded the information to a padd and took it over to Khala.

"Take a look at this, Khala," she said, handing it to the young woman. "Do you know what this is?"

Khala glanced down at the padd, her long fingers curiously caressing its square shape as she read the information.

"Certainly. That's a textbook example of standard molecular structure. In this case, it happens to be my species." She glanced from one to the other. "What's the problem?"

The Doctor frowned and handed her another padd. *"This* is the standard molecular structure with which we're familiar," he said. "In this case, it happens to be Captain Janeway's."

Khala looked down at the schematic and her eyes widened. "That's impossible." She looked at them, angry and confused. "Your humor is difficult for me to understand."

Janeway shook her head. "No joke, Khala."

"But then . . . What's going on?" asked the woman. "You are completely unlike any life-form I've ever heard of!"

"Mutual," said the Doctor. "Ah, I love a mystery."

Although it seemed that everybody wanted a piece of her, Janeway could delay her task no longer. She returned to the bridge and slipped into her chair.

For a moment, she looked around, taking it in, letting it settle in her mind. Tuvok was at his post, capable as always. Both he and Seven of Nine, who was presently down in engineering, had survived the encounter that had claimed Ensign Kirby and Lieutenant Ramirez. For that, at least, she was glad. Kim was down in sickbay. The two science stations were manned, and the conn was occupied by the capable Ensign Jenkins.

She missed seeing Tom's long, lean form there, hearing his quips that were just this side of insubordination. And oh, the empty chair at her left side was a palpable ache. She had come to rely so much on Chakotay, on his quiet good humor and cool head. He, of all of them, would most relish this new adventure upon which they were about to embark.

But she trusted Tialin, on a cell-deep level that she could not articulate. Somehow, they were where they needed to be. She could only hope that someday they would be permitted to rejoin her crew. In the meantime, they would have to press on, though the bridge would not be the same without the presence of these two vital men.

Janeway took a deep breath, opened a shipwide channel and hit the controls.

"This is Captain Janeway. Please cease activity for a moment and give your full attention to this announcement. I'm certain that the rumors are flying and I want everyone to be apprised of our present status.

"You all know that we were victorious in our battle with the Romulans, though we regret the unnecessary loss of life that ensued. The away team was successful in making contact with one of the Shepherds. She gave us the technology to extract the mutated dark matter from this vessel and contain it safely."

She smothered a smile as she could hear faint whoops from various parts of the ship.

"Lieutenant Torres, Seven of Nine, and our honored guest Telek R'Mor are hard at work getting that technology up and running. I've no doubt that they will succeed." She paused a moment before continuing. "While on the planet, Commander Chakotay and Ensign Thomas Eugene Paris disappeared into a portal that led elsewhere. We do not know where they are, but the Shepherd has given me her assurance that they are not in immediate danger. I have high hopes that they will be returned to us. In the meantime, I consider them alive and well and doing Federation-sanctioned work wherever they are. There will be no speculations otherwise.

"We have taken aboard a visitor named Shamraa Khala Remilkansuur. She is presently in sickbay being examined by the Doctor. Once she is released, I hope all of you will make her feel welcome. Khala may be with us for quite some time."

Again Janeway paused, reaching for the words. "While we were on the planet with the Shepherd, I agreed to assist her in a certain . . . quest. We know firsthand how devastating the mutated dark matter can be. It has taken the lives of some of us, driven others of us mad, and threatened to destroy *Voyager* itself. I have learned that there is more of this deadly matter scattered throughout the quadrant. It is destroying other worlds even as I speak to you.

"The Shepherd Tialin has given us the technology to contain and render harmless this lethal matter, and has asked me to take *Voyager* to various infected systems and offer our assistance. On behalf of this crew, I accepted the challenge. It will delay our journey home, but thanks to Telek R'Mor's wormhole technology we will get where we need to go quickly and efficiently. And if we can work out the glitches, who knows but that, when this is all over, we might even be able to go home at last."

She took a breath before continuing. "Millions of lives are depending on us. I know that every one of you is up to this challenge and would not choose to shrink from it."

She smiled softly, her eyes unfocused, imagining the future. "It's going to be a hell of a ride."

EPILOGUE

THE SENATE WAS IN CHAOS.

So much, Jekri had known to expect. Several of their number had not made it back; in fact, only one, pale-faced and shaking with what she graciously decided to consider outrage, had rejoined his fellows. He now sat at a place of honor, a flask of blue ale at his side from which he quaffed perhaps more often than was seemly. But then, given the circumstances, she supposed she couldn't blame him.

The surviving warbird had sent ahead the record, of course. They viewed it in silence, hearing the slight beeping noise that had alerted all the ships that *Voyager* was trying to make contact. For the briefest of instants, Jekri wondered what the hated Captain Janeway had been about in trying to hail them. A trick? For what purpose? Clearly the Federation vessel had been far superior to the warbirds. As Verrak had pointed out, no trickery had been needed to blow them out of the skies.

Jekri swallowed hard as she watched ship after ship being destroyed. Worst of all was when one ship would explode and take its nearest comrade with it.

"The damn wormholes," Lhiau breathed, standing beside her. "Something in there is destroying the ships."

The Little Dagger was reckoned unusually strong of will even by the standards of her own people, a race for whom will was considered a primary virtue. She clamped down hard on the thought that led to Lhiau and not to Telek R'Mor, and forced her mind to agree with the Shepherd's statement: *Something must have gone wrong inside the wormhole. Something Telek R'Mor didn't count on, or wasn't aware of. Surely that was it.*

It was the Empress's raw grief that moved Jekri more than the shouts and accusations of the Senate, the Praetor, and the Proconsul. The Empress had been crying. Her eyes were bloodshot, pale green tendrils twining around the dark irises. Her color was high as well, and when she spoke, her voice was thick.

"What went wrong?" she demanded.

"The Tal Shiar, our top scientists, and the military are conducting a joint investigation into the incident," replied Jekri with as much calm as she could muster. "We shall report to you the minute we know anything."

"No," the Empress said, her voice icy. "No, you

shall report to me hourly, Little Dagger, or I shall know why. We have lost all but one of our cloaked vessels. They seemed to be more vulnerable than they should have been, given what we know of *Voyager*."

Still acutely aware of the towering presence of Lhiau at her side, Jekri replied, "Perhaps we did not know everything about the Federation vessel. Careful scrutiny of the records will teach us more. We will be better prepared for it next time, I promise you, Your Excellency."

The Empress was still not placated. "The alleged superiority of the Federation vessel aside, I demand to know why our ships exploded so easily. It seemed as though they passed destruction from warbird to warbird, like some kind of evil contamination."

Lhiau interrupted before Jekri could even draw breath to speak. "It is my belief that there was something harmful inside the wormhole, something Telek R'Mor either created or hid from his Empire. Something that weakened the dark-matter shields and the vessels. Rest assured, Your Excellency, I shall not sleep until this mystery is solved!"

He looked every inch the nobleman. Gone was the sneer on the handsome face, replaced now by an intense glow that was far more false than the honest contempt he had displayed hitherto. Jekri liked the old Lhiau better. She trusted the sneer more than the set jaw.

"I do not think your kind requires sleep," said the Empress archly, "but I accept your commitment. Remember, our ability to help you, Ambassador, hinges on how well you help us first. Thus far, all we have achieved is the loss of twelve cloaked warbirds and hundreds of our noble warriors. We must—we shall—do better next time."

As abruptly as that, the transmission ended. Jekri thought she'd gotten off very easily.

After speaking with her people, the scientists and military personnel assigned to this operation, Jekri headed for the privacy of Telek R'Mor's room. Lhiau was nowhere on the *Talvath*, but Jekri wasn't about to let her guard down, not now, when it was so important.

So she stepped into the sonic shower, letting her hands caress her body, and deliberately filled her head with thoughts of Verrak: of his keen mind, his unexpected humor, his quick reactions. His hands, his face, his strong, toned, warrior's body. Jekri stepped out of the shower and dressed in the softest, most revealing clothes she had. It was a dress comprised of several layers, worn on those rare state occasions when the chairman of the Tal Shiar needed to be seen as just another Romulan citizen enjoying a meal, or art, or some other such nonsensical time-waster. Jekri donned only a few of the layers. The effect was that the clothing was almost transparent, precisely what she wanted.

Verrak. She imagined his hands touching her, of being locked in the most intimate of embraces. She sat down at the small screen in the bedroom and sent a message to Verrak, who was in his quarters on another vessel.

"Subcommander Verrak. Chairman Kaleh," he

said, surprise creeping into his voice. He couldn't see all of her, but she had let the first draping slip off one creamy shoulder. Jekri smiled at him, her silver eyes peeking through lowered lashes.

"Verrak," she said, her voice husky. "I need to see you. In private. Will you transport over to the *Talvath?*"

She saw him swallow hard. "At once, Chairman."

And indeed, it was but a moment later that he materialized in her room, in full uniform still, looking very ill at ease and peculiarly, absurdly shy.

Jekri rose, went to him, draped her arms about his neck and kissed him deeply. He was tense in her embrace at first, then all at once yielded and took control at the same moment, his arms like iron bands around her body.

Jekri broke the kiss. In the faintest of whispers, she said, "Lhiau knows how to read thoughts. He is not on board, but we don't know what kind of being he truly is. I needed to fill our thoughts with distracting images before we spoke of our true mission."

Verrak's green-flushed face went still. "Of course, Chairman. An excellent ruse."

They both knew that he had thought it no ruse, and for the briefest of moments, Jekri felt sorry for the deception. For an even briefer instant, she wished that this scenario were as simple as a woman seducing a man. Especially this man.

She pulled on his uniform, taking him to the bed. She kissed him again, but his lips were still against hers. "I do not think there is anything wrong inside the wormhole, Verrak," she said softly. "I begin to believe you. Perhaps this Telek R'Mor is no traitor after all."

"You do me honor, Chairman." Verrak seemed to need to lace every reference to her with her title. He wanted the distance, Jekri realized.

"Lhiau is not showing us his true face," she continued. "We need to begin our own investigation, you and I, into these Shepherds and their technology. All is not what it seems."

Verrak pulled away from her on the bed, one hand reaching as if compelled to stroke her cheek with a profound gentleness before clenching into a fist.

"I agree, Chairman. Where do we begin?"

They lay on the bed, whispering like lovers, and began to plot.

About the Author

Christie Golden is the author of thirteen novels and fourteen short stories. Among her credits are three other *Voyager* novels, *The Murdered Sun, Marooned,* and *Seven of Nine,* as well as a Tom Paris short story, "A Night at Sandrine's," for *Amazing Stories.* On the strength of *The Murdered Sun,* Golden now has an open invitation to pitch for *Voyager,* the show.

In addition to *Star Trek* novels, Golden has also written three original fantasy novels, *Instrument of Fate, King's Man and Thief,* and, under the pen name Jadrien Bell, *A.D. 999.*

Golden lives in Colorado with her husband, two cats, and a white German shepherd. Readers are encouraged to visit her website at www.sff.net/people/Christie.Golden.

Look for STAR TREK fiction from Pocket Books

Star Trek®: The Original Series

Star Trek: The Next Generation®

#24-26 • *Rebels* • Dafydd ab Hugh
    #24 • *The Conquered*
    #25 • *The Courageous*
    #26 • *The Liberated*

Star Trek: Voyager®

    Mosaic • Jeri Taylor
    Pathways • Jeri Taylor
    Captain Proton! • Dean Wesley Smith
Novelizations
    Caretaker • L.A. Graf
    Flashback • Diane Carey
    Day of Honor • Michael Jan Friedman
    Equinox • Diane Carey

  #1 • *Caretaker* • L.A. Graf
  #2 • *The Escape* • Dean Wesley Smith & Kristine Kathryn Rusch
  #3 • *Ragnarok* • Nathan Archer
  #4 • *Violations* • Susan Wright
  #5 • *Incident at Arbuk* • John Gregory Betancourt
  #6 • *The Murdered Sun* • Christie Golden
  #7 • *Ghost of a Chance* • Mark A. Garland & Charles G. McGraw
  #8 • *Cybersong* • S.N. Lewitt
  #9 • *Invasion! #4: Final Fury* • Dafydd ab Hugh
#10 • *Bless the Beasts* • Karen Haber
#11 • *The Garden* • Melissa Scott
#12 • *Chrysalis* • David Niall Wilson
#13 • *The Black Shore* • Greg Cox
#14 • *Marooned* • Christie Golden
#15 • *Echoes* • Dean Wesley Smith, Kristine Kathryn Rusch &
    Nina Kiriki Hoffman
#16 • *Seven of Nine* • Christie Golden
#17 • *Death of a Neutron Star* • Eric Kotani
#18 • *Battle Lines* • Dave Galanter & Greg Brodeur

Star Trek®: New Frontier

New Frontier #1-4 Collector's Edition • Peter David
#1 • *House of Cards* • Peter David
#2 • *Into the Void* • Peter David
#3 • *The Two-Front War* • Peter David

#4 • *End Game* • Peter David
#5 • *Martyr* • Peter David
#6 • *Fire on High* • Peter David
The Captain's Table #5 • *Once Burned* • Peter David
Double Helix #5 • *Double or Nothing* • Peter David
#7 • *The Quiet Place* • Peter David
#8 • *Dark Allies* • Peter David

Star Trek®: Invasion!

#1 • *First Strike* • Diane Carey
#2 • *The Soldiers of Fear* • Dean Wesley Smith & Kristine Kathryn Rusch
#3 • *Time's Enemy* • L.A. Graf
#4 • *Final Fury* • Dafydd ab Hugh
Invasion! Omnibus • various

Star Trek®: Day of Honor

#1 • *Ancient Blood* • Diane Carey
#2 • *Armageddon Sky* • L.A. Graf
#3 • *Her Klingon Soul* • Michael Jan Friedman
#4 • *Treaty's Law* • Dean Wesley Smith & Kristine Kathryn Rusch
The Television Episode • Michael Jan Friedman
Day of Honor Omnibus • various

Star Trek®: The Captain's Table

#1 • *War Dragons* • L.A. Graf
#2 • *Dujonian's Hoard* • Michael Jan Friedman
#3 • *The Mist* • Dean Wesley Smith & Kristine Kathryn Rusch
#4 • *Fire Ship* • Diane Carey
#5 • *Once Burned* • Peter David
#6 • *Where Sea Meets Sky* • Jerry Oltion

Star Trek®: The Dominion War

#1 • *Behind Enemy Lines* • John Vornholt
#2 • *Call to Arms...* • Diane Carey
#3 • *Tunnel Through the Stars* • John Vornholt
#4 • *...Sacrifice of Angels* • Diane Carey

Star Trek® Books available in Trade Paperback

Omnibus Editions
   Invasion! Omnibus • various
   Day of Honor Omnibus • various
   The Captain's Table Omnibus • various
   Star Trek: Odyssey • William Shatner with Judith and Garfield
      Reeves-Stevens
Other Books
   Legends of the Ferengi • Ira Steven Behr & Robert Hewitt Wolfe
   Strange New Worlds, vol. I and II • Dean Wesley Smith, ed.
   Adventures in Time and Space • Mary Taylor
   The Lives of Dax • Marco Palmieri, ed.
   Captain Proton! • Dean Wesley Smith

STAR TREK
THE EXPERIENCE
LAS VEGAS HILTON

Be a part of the most exciting deep space adventure in the galaxy as you beam aboard the U.S.S. Enterprise. Explore the evolution of Star Trek® from television to movies in the "History of the Future Museum," the planet's largest collection of authentic Star Trek memorabilia. Then, visit distant galaxies on the "Voyage Through Space." This 22-minute action packed adventure will capture your senses with the latest in motion simulator technology. After your mission, shop in the Deep Space Nine Promenade and enjoy 24th Century cuisine in Quark's Bar & Restaurant.

Save up to $30